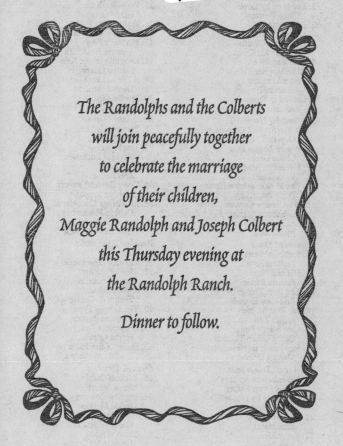

The Randolphs and the Colberts
will join peacefully together
to celebrate the marriage
of their children,
Maggie Randolph and Joseph Colbert
this Thursday evening at
the Randolph Ranch.

Dinner to follow.

Please address questions and book requests to: Silhouette Reader Service
U.S.: 3010 Walden Ave., P.O. Box 1325, Buffalo, NY 14269
Canadian: P.O. Box 609, Fort Erie, Ont. L2A 5X3

WESTERN *Lovers*

ELIZABETH AUGUST

WILD HORSE CANYON

Published by Silhouette Books

America's Publisher of Contemporary Romance

 **SILHOUETTE BOOKS**
300 East 42nd St.,
New York, N.Y. 10017

ISBN 0-373-88511-3

WILD HORSE CANYON

Chapter One

Frank Randolph lay on his deathbed. He was bullheaded and cantankerous, but he was also Maggie's only family, and she loved him. She would have given her life for his if she could, but God didn't make deals like that.

Lying propped up on pillows, Frank watched his granddaughter enter his bedroom and approach his bed. She was dressed in patched jeans, a plaid shirt and cowboy boots ready for a hard day's work on the ranch. "Stu Gibson is coming for lunch today," he said with a firmness that belied his critical condition. "I want you here, looking pretty and feminine."

Maggie was willing to die for her grandfather but she wasn't willing to put up with his matchmaking. "I don't have time to have lunch with you and Stu. It's spring and the fences need to be checked for repairs, not to mention making an accurate count of our cattle and rounding up the new calves."

"You can tell Chester what you want done and he'll see it gets done," Frank ordered. "That's what foremen are for and Chester's one of the best. I trained him myself."

Maggie spread her feet slightly and stiffened her back, as she prepared to stand her ground. "You know I like to check on things myself. That's something you taught *me*."

Frank's jaw hardened. "I want you here." He spoke with the authority of a man who was used to having his commands obeyed without question.

Maggie's green eyes narrowed in exasperation. Then, drawing a tired sigh, she said in a reasoning tone, "Let's be honest with each other. You want me here so you can do a little matchmaking . . . no, make that a lot of matchmaking, and I don't want to be matched.''

Frank's voice undertook a reasoning tone, too. ''I'm worried about you. When I'm gone, you'll be all alone in the world. You've had your one great love match. I'm sorry I didn't treat Sam better. I'm sorry you had to run away to get married. I'm sorry he died so young. But that's in the past and I can't undo what's been done. It's time to be practical.'' He motioned for her to come sit on the side of his bed. ''You're twenty-seven,'' he continued, taking her hand in his as she seated herself beside him. ''That's not ancient, but if you're going to have children you need to get started. It may be selfish of me but I'd like to think that Randolph blood will run through the veins of the future owners of the Double R.''

Maggie wanted to assure her grandfather that this would come to pass, but she couldn't. The thought of an intimate relationship with any man left her cold.

Frank frowned at her silence. ''You've been widowed for nine years; it's time for you to get on with your life.''

''I am getting on with my life,'' she insisted.

"No, you're not!" Frustration mingled with the concern in his voice. "You're living with a ghost and that ain't healthy."

Maggie's jaw hardened. "I have a right to live my life as I see fit."

As he drew a terse breath, Frank's expression became grim. "Stu wants to buy the Double R, and I'm thinking of selling it to him."

Maggie's eyes rounded in shock. "No!"

"You love this ranch as much as you loved Sam Hagan," Frank explained curtly. "I figure you'll marry Stu to keep it."

"That's blackmail!" Jerking free of her grandfather's hold, she rose and glared down at him. "I can't believe you would do this to me!"

"Stu's a good man. He'll take good care of you."

"Stu Gibson is nearly twice my age," she pointed out curtly.

"He's only in his early forties," Frank corrected.

"He's boring," she stated frankly, "and he's still in love with his dead wife. He's got her pictures all over the house. It's like the entire place is a shrine to her. Everyone knows the only reason he wants to marry is to sire the children she was never able to give him."

"Then you'll both be on equal ground," Frank replied.

Maggie was frantic. She knew her grandfather well and the determined look on his face left no doubt that he was deadly serious. She had to think quickly. A plan formed in her mind. It wasn't a particularly nice thing to do to a dying man, but she was desperate. This ranch was her home; other than her grandfather, it was the only stable force in her life. She felt safe here. But the feeling went even deeper than that. This ranch was as much a part of her as one of her arms or legs. Forcing calmness into her voice, she asked, "Do you simply want me married or have you decided that I must marry Stu Gibson?"

"I want you married to a man I know will take good care of you," Frank answered.

Maggie's jaw tensed. "And that's your only requirement?"

Frank scowled. "Not the only one."

"What are the rest of them?" she demanded.

"This is for your own good," he said stiffly, resolve etched deeply into his features. "He has to be solid—a man who is levelheaded, hard-working and who understands the importance of family. He also has to love this land and be willing to put his own sweat into it. In other words, I want a man with a rancher's heart who's willing to settle down with a wife and raise a family."

What he wants is someone who's entirely different from Sam Hagan, my rodeo-star first husband, Maggie noted mentally. With a touch of sarcasm, she said, "You don't think you're asking too much, do you?"

Frank regarded her thoughtfully. "And he has to be a man with a strong will. You've got your grandmother's red hair and the temper that goes with it."

Maggie raked a hand through her thick coppery tresses in an agitated manner. "Is that all?" she asked dryly.

Frank's voice was coaxing. "I know you don't want to fall in love again. I'm not asking you to do that. I'm asking you to take a practical step. Marry so there will be heirs for our land and so I won't have to worry about you going through life alone."

"And if I find someone who answers that description and am willing to marry him, you'll leave the Double R to me?" she asked.

"You'll have to find him soon," Frank stipulated. "I want to see you married before my time is up."

Maggie didn't like what she was about to do, but he'd left her no choice. "The ranch is mine if I find a man who fits your requirements and I'm willing to marry him," she restated the bargain.

Frank nodded.

"Shake on it," she said, extending her hand.

As her grandfather's hand closed about hers, Maggie drew a shaky breath. So far her plan was working. Her grandfather's handshake was his bond. Now came the hard part. "There is someone I've been seeing who fits that description."

Frank stared at her in disbelief. "You've been seeing a man?"

Maggie looked properly embarrassed and uneasy. "He's even asked me to marry him, but I refused. I love him, but I knew you would fight the match with all the strength you could muster."

"Who is it?" Frank demanded blackly.

Maggie straightened her shoulders. "Joe Colbert," she said, then waited, barely breathing. She was certain her grandfather would refuse to allow this match and then she would win this battle. She would retain her freedom and the Double R would still be hers. Their agreement was that she find a man she was willing to marry, not that she actually marry him.

But the anger Maggie had expected to see reflected on her grandfather's face was missing. "Joe Colbert." He repeated the name as if he needed to hear himself say it to really believe it. "I always wondered why he hadn't married yet. The Colberts are strong family people. Been waiting for you, has he?" Frank mused. Then a speculative glimmer shone in his eyes. "Uniting the White Stallion Ranch and the Double R ain't a bad idea. Can't say I find it easy to trust a Colbert but if you really love him, I won't stand in your way."

Maggie couldn't believe her ears. The Colberts and the Randolphs had been feuding for four generations. Over the years they had accused one another of trespassing and cattle rustling. They were constantly arguing over boundaries and water rights.

Then there was Wild Horse Canyon. It housed
a nice-size spring, and water was a precious
commodity in west Texas. The Colberts had always considered the canyon part of their ranch,
but eleven years ago, Maggie's grandfather found
an old land claim that seemed to support his
contention that Wild Horse Canyon belonged to
the Randolphs. Frank took Karl Colbert, Joe's
grandfather, to court and won. The Colberts had
called Frank a land-grabbing old thief and Frank
responded by refusing to allow the Colbert name
to be mentioned in his home. A few years ago,
Karl died and Joe inherited the ranch and the
position as her grandfather's number one enemy. Now Frank was actually considering accepting him as a grandson-in-law.

An authoritative knock on the door broke the
heavy silence in the bedroom. Jane Kert, Frank's
private-duty nurse, briskly entered. Jane was in
her early forties, tall and slender with blond hair.
She had a nice face and a reassuring smile, but
behind the pleasant countenance was a will of
iron. She'd nursed the cowboys in and around
the Pecos area for twenty years and she refused
to be bullied by any of them, including Frank
Randolph. "It's time for your grandfather's

medication and nap," she announced in a voice that would tolerate no dissention.

"Good idea," Maggie muttered. Giving her grandfather a kiss on the cheek, she quickly escaped into the hall.

How am I going to get out of this? she thought frantically as she left the house. Walking to the stables, she considered several ploys, finally settling for the simplest. She'd say that she and Joe had a fight, but she still loved him and knew they would get back together once the dust settled. That would give her some time to come up with a better solution.

Confident that she had the situation under control, Maggie concentrated on her work around the ranch.

It was a couple of hours later, while she was helping one of the ranch hands repair the gate on one of the nearby corrals, that Sarah came hurrying toward her. Sarah Martin had been the housekeeper at the Double R since before Maggie was born. She had a gentle, mothering soul and had been Maggie's primary source of comfort when her parents died. Seeing the fifty-year-old woman coming toward her at a jogging gait, Maggie froze in fear. She knew her grandfather's time was close but she wasn't ready for it to come today.

"You'd better come quick!" Sarah said between gasps as she reached Maggie. "Joe Colbert just arrived and went up to your grandfather's room."

Maggie's relief that her grandfather hadn't gone to meet his maker lasted only a moment before a cold sweat broke out on her brow. "Joe Colbert?"

Sarah nodded. "I tried to stop him, but he said he's a busy man. He said the only reason he's here is because Frank called and said he had something real important he wanted to talk to him about and it couldn't wait. Joe said he didn't like being here any more than I liked him being here, but he figured since Frank's on his deathbed, he ought to allow him this one last request."

Forgetting about the gate, Maggie started toward the house at a fast clip.

"Now, mind you," Sarah continued, trying to keep pace. "I don't mind Joe Colbert. I've always thought this feud has gone too far, but I don't want your grandfather getting himself upset."

Maggie broke into a jog, leaving Sarah panting for breath behind her. She was afraid to even think about her grandfather's reaction when he found out that she'd lied to him.

"I'm going to unplug your grandfather's phone," Jane said seethingly as Maggie came flying up the stairs. The nurse was standing in the hall glaring at the closed bedroom door. "Frank promised me he would take his nap, and the minute my back was turned he called Joe Colbert." A strong note of apology entered her voice. "I tried to stop them but when your grandfather and Joe Colbert have their minds set on a confrontation, it's like trying to stop two runaway locomotives!" Indignation flashed in Jane's eyes. "Frank ordered me out of the room and when I refused to leave, Joe actually carried me into the hall. Then he went back inside and locked the door."

"I know you did your best," Maggie assured her. Approaching the bedroom door, she pounded on it. "Let me in!" she demanded. She didn't really want to face either man, but she had to know what was being said.

A moment later the lock clicked and the door opened. "Come in, darlin'," Joe said.

His clothes were dusty and he smelled of horses and sweat. His thick, dark brown hair still showed a ring of wetness where the hatband of his old gray Stetson had been. Obviously, he had wasted no time in answering her grandfather's summons. A flush of embarrassment spread upward from Maggie's neck. There was a smile on his ruggedly handsome face but it didn't reach the dark brown eyes that regarded her suspiciously. Her pride demanded that she not let this cowboy intimidate her, but it wasn't easy. He had an unquestionable air of authority. Then there was his physical presence. His six-foot-two bulk dwarfed her five-foot-seven frame. His shoulders and chest were broad and strong from years of hard work, and his faded jeans hugged his muscular thighs.

Slipping an arm around her waist, he drew her into the room, then closed and locked the door. "Your grandfather's been telling me how you love me and want to marry me. He says the only reason you rejected my proposals is because you didn't want to upset him." Joe's brown eyes seemed almost black. He studied her with a what-game-are-you-playing look.

Maggie couldn't think of anything to say, and even if she did, she wasn't certain her vocal cords would work. Joe was keeping his arm around her, holding her captive. She expected to feel repulsed by his touch, but the granitelike strength of his arm was causing an excitement to stir within her. *I'm just anxious about Gramps finding out I lied,* she reasoned. For the past nine years she'd been immune to men and she wasn't ready to believe Joe Colbert's touch could affect her so easily.

"I've been explaining to Joe that for your sake, I'm willing to call an end to this feud," Frank said. "I'd like to see the two of you married before I die."

"We've been discussing terms." Joe's gaze narrowed on Maggie as if he were trying to read her mind. "Your grandfather has explained that he plans to have his will drawn up leaving the Double R to you exclusively. He wants me to sign a prenuptial agreement stipulating that if our marriage doesn't work, I won't try to get my hands on your inheritance. In other words, he wants to be certain I'm marrying you for love, not your ranch."

"Sounds reasonable," she managed to say, stalling for time. Obviously Joe hadn't given her lie away. She wondered why, but there was no clue in the dark eyes that continued to study her with an unnerving intensity.

"Then it's settled," Joe said gruffly. The arm around her waist tightened possessively, pulling Maggie to him. In the next moment his mouth found hers.

Instinctively, Maggie's hands rose to push him away. Then she remembered her grandfather's presence and let them rest nondefensively on Joe's chest. Still, her body braced against the expected unpleasantness of the encounter. But to her shock there was nothing unpleasant about it. Joe's lips were firm but gentle and there was a coaxing quality in his kiss as if he were trying to entice her to respond. What really disquieted her was that her body answered. Unconsciously she moved closer to him, and a hot, curling sensation spread through her abdomen. Startled and unnerved, she reminded herself that according to the gossip, Joe Colbert had a great deal of experience with women. He knew how to make them respond.

Maggie saw the glimmer of satisfaction in his eyes as he raised his head from hers, and her body stiffened away from him. Furious with herself for practically melting in his arms, she forced a coolness into her eyes to suggest that this had all been a show for her grandfather.

Shifting his gaze away from her and toward the bed, Joe said levelly, "If you'll excuse us, we have wedding plans to make."

"You two run along." Frank smiled broadly, looking as if a weight had been lifted from his shoulders. "And you can tell that nurse of mine she can rest easy now. I'm going to take that nap she ordered."

Maggie forced a returning smile as she and Joe left the room. Out in the hall Sarah and Jane were waiting. Both women greeted Joe with hostile glares, letting him know that if he'd upset Frank, he wasn't safe in their presence.

"Everything's fine," Maggie assured them. Turning to Jane, she added, "My grandfather is taking the nap you prescribed."

"And Maggie and I are going into the study for a private conversation. We don't want to be disturbed," Joe said firmly.

Immediately Sarah's and Jane's attitude became one of defense for Maggie.

"I really would appreciate it if you'd see that we aren't disturbed," Maggie said with a calm she didn't feel.

"If that's what you want," Sarah agreed, studying Maggie with puzzled concern. "But if you need me I'll be within shouting distance." She emphasized this last statement with a warning glance at Joe.

A mischievous grin played at the corners of his mouth. "I promise to behave like a gentleman," he assured the housekeeper, "I know better than to tangle with you."

Maggie saw Sarah flush with pleasure. The Colbert charm, she mused dryly, was certainly strong.

Very strong, a little voice within her agreed. Joe was holding on to her arm as if he thought she might try to bolt and, to her chagrin, his touch was sending tiny rivulets of warmth coursing through her. Unnerved by her body's reaction to him, she wanted to jerk free but couldn't in front of Sarah and Jane. Again, telling herself this physical response was only due to her worry about the lie she'd told her grandfather, she forced herself to maintain a cool exterior and walk calmly with him to the study. Once they were in the room, she didn't need to jerk away.

Kicking the door shut, he released her abruptly. Then pacing across the floor, he put a good six feet between them before he turned to face her. "Now I think it's time you told me what's going on here," he said grimly.

Maggie studied him guardedly. Joe was two years older than she was, and in a way she could say she had known him all her life. His parents raised him in Houston, but he'd spent nearly every summer on the White Stallion Ranch with his grandfather. His older brother had followed in his father's footsteps and became a lawyer, but Joe had studied animal husbandry in college and come to the ranch to work with his grandfather after graduation. When Karl Colbert died, it seemed only natural that he would leave his ranch to Joe. But although Maggie and Joe were neighbors, the feud was a strong barrier between them and through the years that barrier had grown even stronger. She didn't know him well enough to be certain what kind of a reaction to expect from him.

"I want an explanation," he demanded impatiently when her hesitation lengthened into a silence.

"It's really none of your concern," she said stiffly. "It would be best if you just went home and forgot about this."

"Your grandfather called me over here because he got the idea in his head that I want to marry you. Then you come in and kiss me as if it's true."

"You kissed me!" she corrected curtly.

He shrugged a shoulder as if to say it made no difference who had initiated the kiss. Then the frown on his face deepening, he continued tersely, "I'm pretty certain I just struck a bargain with your grandfather for your hand in marriage. Now you tell me it's none of my concern."

He didn't have to make marriage to her sound so distasteful. "You didn't have to play along with him," she snapped.

"He might be a Randolph but he *is* on his deathbed. I didn't want to upset him," he replied in clipped tones. "Before you came into the room, I hadn't confirmed anything he said, I simply hadn't denied it. Then you came in and played along. Knowing how much you dislike my company, I figured there must be a hell of a strong reason for you to let the lie stand. So I continued to go along with it. But now I want to know what that reason is, and I'm not leaving until you tell me.''

Joe's stance and the expression on his face made it clear that he meant business. Well, if the truth would get rid of him, she'd give it to him. She just wanted him gone. Clearing her throat, she faced him levelly. ''My grandfather has suddenly become overly anxious about my future and the future of the Randolph bloodline. He...'' She stopped as embarrassment tightened her throat. She couldn't tell Joe Colbert what had gone on between her and Frank. She'd never live down the humiliation. Swallowing, she continued stiffly, ''This really isn't your problem. It would be best for all of us if you would just go back to your ranch and forget this morning ever happened.''

Joe's gaze narrowed threateningly. ''You're wrong, Maggie. Your grandfather is under the impression that I'm in line to be his grandson-in-law, and I want to know why.''

Maggie forced a nonchalance into her manner. "My grandfather is ill. He's not accountable for what he thinks these days." Moving toward the door, she said over her shoulder, "Now I would like you to leave."

Crossing the room in long strides, Joe caught her wrist as she reached for the doorknob. "Not so fast." Anger mingled with impatience in his voice. His grip on her wrist tightened and he jerked her around to face him. "Do you know how the feud between our families got started?" he growled.

Fighting back a rush of fear, Maggie faced him defiantly. "It had something to do with a woman."

"That's exactly right," he growled. "Our great-grandfathers started out as friends. They'd known each other since they were boys. Then a woman came into their lives. She played them both for suckers and ran off with another man. They were both too embarrassed to admit they'd been made fools of by a woman so they blamed each other for what had happened and the feud began." Joe's jaw hardened. "I don't like it when women play games, Maggie. They don't play fair and they stir up a storm of trouble for everyone."

"This isn't a game!" Jerking free, Maggie backed away from him. With most men she had no problem maintaining control, but Joe Colbert unnerved her. Her wrist still felt hot from his touch and, unconsciously she rubbed it, trying to rid herself of the disturbing sensation.

The action wasn't lost on Joe. "I didn't mean to hurt you," he apologized gruffly.

Following his line of vision, Maggie saw herself rubbing her wrist and immediately stopped. "You didn't," she muttered. Then in firmer tones, she added, "Would you please just leave?"

Leaning against the door, he crossed his arms in front of his chest and regarded her purposefully. "Neither of us is leaving this room until you tell me what's going on."

Maggie hated the way those dark eyes of his seemed almost capable of boring into her innermost thoughts. She felt desperate to be rid of him. "All right, have it your way." She raked a hand through her hair then, hooking her thumbs in the pockets of her jeans, she faced him with proud defiance. "My grandfather suddenly decided that I should marry. He even chose a husband...Stu Gibson. When I refused to consider the match, he threatened to sell the Double R to Stu. He knows how much this ranch means to me and he figured I'd marry Stu to keep it." Maggie felt an uncontrollable flush of embarrassment begin to build in her cheeks. Her chin tightened with righteous indignation. "I don't take well to being blackmailed. I got my grandfather to list the qualities he wanted in the man I married and to agree that if I found a man who met those requirements and I was willing to marry him, I could have the ranch. Then I named you. I said we'd been seeing each other behind his back because I knew he wouldn't approve and I didn't want him upset when he was so sick. I was certain he would refuse to consider the match. But since I'd met my part of the bargain, the ranch would be mine."

A cynical smile played at the corners of Joe's mouth. "An interesting ploy. But it seems to have backfired."

Maggie's embarrassed flush turned to anger. He was laughing at her. "The doctors don't give

Gramps more than a month longer to live.'' She paused as this statement caused hot tears to suddenly burn behind her eyes. Forcing herself to finish, she said tersely, "I'll play for time. I'll tell him that proper weddings can't be arranged in a day."

"He's tough as boot leather. He could be around a lot longer than any doctor can predict," Joe said matter-of-factly.

"I hope so," she murmured as if saying a silent prayer. Even if Gramps had placed her in an extremely uncomfortable position, she wasn't ready to lose him yet. Then because her nerves were beginning to feel positively brittle and she was tired of being a source of amusement for Joe Colbert, she said with dismissal, "I've told you what is going on so now you can leave."

Joe reached for the doorknob, but as his hand made contact, he suddenly turned back to face her. "I don't approve of your grandfather's methods, but he does have a point. You're a good-looking woman, Maggie. It's a shame for you to waste yourself on the memory of a man who's been dead for nine years."

Maggie's jaw tightened. "I don't tell you how to run your life, Joe Colbert. Don't tell me how to run mine."

The cynical smile returned to his face. "Yes, ma'am," he said, and opening the door, he left the study.

Chapter Two

Maggie heard the front door closing and the sound of the motor of Joe's pickup as he started it and drove away. Sinking into a chair, she leaned her head back and closed her eyes. Why in the world did she let Joe Colbert rattle her so badly? *It's not him. It's worrying about my grandfather and trying to cope with this latest demand of his,* she assured herself.

But as she sat trying to calm her nerves, her various encounters with Joe Colbert over the years began to play through her mind. His grandfather had been a firm churchgoer and he'd made Joe go to church with him every Sunday that Joe was at the ranch. But even though Joe and Maggie were in the same Sunday school class, they never talked. No one expected them to. In fact, it would have been the gossip of the week if they had. And it was still that way. Joe still went to church every Sunday and Maggie ignored him, and he ignored her.

Well, she didn't totally ignore him. She did find a certain cynical amusement in watching the unmarried women flirt with him. *You'd think they'd have learned by now,* she mused. He dated periodically but never developed any serious attachments. In spite of her grandfather's belief that Joe was a strong family man, it was clear to Maggie that he preferred independence to marriage.

"And that's probably just as well," she muttered. He was bound to be difficult to live with. He was as arrogant and authoritative as his grandfather.

A frown suddenly wrinkled Maggie's brow. She wasn't exactly being fair. She didn't like to admit it, but she knew Joe could be gentle and understanding when he wanted to be. She vividly recalled the day of her parents' funeral.

They'd died in a plane crash when she was eleven. Still in shock, she'd made it through the service with only a moderate number of tears and afterward she'd put on a brave face for her grandfather's sake. But later that day, when everyone thought she was resting, she slipped away. She'd changed into her jeans then ridden out to a small stream where she and her parents had picnicked many times. She was sitting on a boulder sobbing her heart out when Joe rode up.

"You're on Randolph land," she'd said curtly, wiping frantically at her tears in an attempt to keep him from knowing she'd been crying.

"It's no sin to cry, even for a Randolph," he'd said, dismounting and coming to stand beside her.

Ignoring him, she'd picked up a rock and tossed it into the water. But as the ripples spread out from it, she remembered all the times she and her father had sat on this same boulder and watched similar ripples and the tears began to flow again.

"I just wanted to say I'm real sorry about your parents," he'd said uneasily.

"Thanks," she'd managed.

She had expected him to leave after that but he hadn't. Instead he continued to stand beside the boulder.

She started to ask him to leave but the words never formed. It helped having another human being around, even if it was a Colbert.

When she didn't say anything, he'd sat down beside the boulder and began whittling on a piece of wood. For the next hour, neither spoke. Then as the sun began setting, he rose and dusted himself off. "It'll be dark soon," he'd said. "I'd best be getting you home."

Maggie had stared at him in surprise. "I don't need you to get me home."

"I'm going to ride along, anyway," he'd said simply—and he had.

She'd never told him, but she had felt safer with him riding beside her. *But only because I was feeling so vulnerable,* she thought defensively.

Quickly her mind skipped ahead to a day when she was sixteen. She'd been out riding and her horse had been spooked by a rattler. She'd been thrown and her ankle was badly sprained. Her horse ran away and the pain in her ankle was so unbearable when she tried to walk that she'd been forced to sit and wait for someone to find her. She knew that when her horse returned to the barn without her, her grandfather would send out word that she was missing and all the ranchers and their hands would come looking for her. It was only a matter of time before someone came to her rescue. But to her chagrin, that someone turned out to be Joe. She'd been embarrassed to have been thrown and doubly embarrassed to have been rescued by a Colbert.

"I'm really just fine," she'd assured him haughtily. But when she tried to stand, her ankle refused to hold her weight.

"Did anyone every tell you that you have a definite mulish streak?" he'd asked, shaking his head at her foolhardiness.

She'd scowled at him but made no further attempts to refuse his help. Her ankle was throbbing and all she wanted to do was get home.

He'd fired off two shots with his rifle to let the other searchers know she'd been found, then he'd lifted her up behind his saddle. As they started back toward the Double R, she'd been forced to hold on to him to maintain her balance. His back had stiffened and she'd realized that he was just as uneasy in her company as she was in his. Ashamed of herself for behaving so ungratefully, she'd said tightly, "Thanks for finding me."

"Couldn't leave you out there for coyote bait," he'd replied dryly. "They might have eaten you and all died from stomachaches."

She'd glared at the back of his neck and promised herself she would never be polite to him again.

But the next day, Sarah came up to her room with a bouquet of flowers. "Joe Colbert dropped these by," she'd said, frowning in confusion. "Said something about them being an apology for some crack he'd made about coyotes and stomachaches."

Maggie had chewed on her bottom lip and flushed with pleasure, while Sarah had looked worried. Frank found out about the flowers through Sarah. He always sensed when his housekeeper was worried and he knew just how to needle her into telling him what was upsetting her. He made so many cracks about being allergic to the flowers that Maggie finally gave in and let Sarah throw them away. But not until she had taken out a rose and pressed it. After all, this was her first bouquet—even if it had come from a Colbert.

The doctor had made Maggie stay off her ankle for a week. By the end of that time, she felt as if the walls were closing in on her. The day she was allowed up and out, she packed herself a lunch right after breakfast and went for a ride by the stream where she and her parents had used to picnic. She'd been surprised when Joe showed up.

"Heard you were allowed out today," he'd said. "Doc Jones stopped by the house to check on my granddad's blood pressure and mentioned he'd just come from the Double R."

There had been a softness in his brown eyes that caused butterflies to flutter around in her stomach. After that, they met several times by the stream. At first they were both shy, as if they were uncertain about the feelings that seemed to be developing between them. It was never said, but both knew their families would disapprove if they found out about these meetings.

There were times when Maggie nearly didn't go to meet him. But at the last moment, she'd always given in. She told herself that being friends with him couldn't hurt. But she had been wrong.

Her chin tightened as she remembered their last meeting. They'd met by the stream and then gone for a ride. Joe was in an especially good mood that day. He challenged her to a race and when he won, he demanded a prize.

"A kiss," he'd stipulated when she'd asked what prize he sought.

Blushing, she'd agreed. It was her first kiss and while it had been very innocent, she'd felt it all the way to her toes.

"I think it's time we told our families about us," he'd said and she'd agreed. She was so lost in her first real infatuation, she would have agreed to anything.

But they never had told their families. Her grandfather had found the old claim to Wild Horse Canyon that very day and by the next morning he was in court demanding the property.

She'd ridden out to see Joe and he had been there. But almost immediately they started to argue. Each one was certain that their own grandfather was in the right. They'd parted in anger.

Maggie had cried herself to sleep that night. The next day, she'd ridden out to their usual meeting place. Joe was there, but they weren't Maggie and Joe any longer; they were a Colbert and a Randolph with three generations of feuding creating a solid barrier between them. They'd never met there again after that day.

She'd told herself it would be easy to get over him. But it hadn't been. She'd felt the pain for a long time. Then Sam Hagan had come into her life.

Maggie raked her hands through her hair. She didn't want to think about Sam right now. This day had been difficult enough already. Closing her eyes, she remembered the next time she and Joe spoke after their argument over Wild Horse Canyon.

It was five years later . . . five very long years later. In that time she'd married Sam Hagan and been widowed. It was the day of Karl Colbert's funeral. She hadn't been able to get Joe off her mind all that day. She knew how much he loved his grandfather and she recalled the day her parents died. While she didn't like to admit it, his being with her had helped. Early evening came and in an effort to fight off the restlessness she was feeling, she'd gone for a ride. She hadn't thought about where she was going until she reached Colbert land. Then telling herself that she was only paying a duty call because Joe had come to see her when her parents died, she continued toward his home. But as she neared the ranch it occurred to her that there would be a lot of people there from the funeral and she was still wearing her work clothes. And she was a Randolph. That was certain to cause a disruption he wouldn't appreciate. She'd started to turn back when she saw a lone rider coming her way. Even before she could clearly see him, she'd known it was Joe.

"I came to offer my condolences," she said when he reined his horse in next to hers.

"Thanks," he'd replied. He'd looked tired and drawn. With a shrug of his shoulder in the direction of the ranch house, he'd added, "I needed to get away."

She nodded. "I understand."

His dark eyes had looked hard into hers. "I'm glad you came," he'd said gruffly.

Suddenly lost in the deep brown depths of his eyes, she'd felt his pain as if it were her own, and the urge to reach out and put her arms around

him was incredibly strong. Shocked by this reaction, she'd pulled her gaze abruptly away and
an uncomfortable silence had fallen between
them.

Breaking the silence, he'd said with a tired
scowl, "I'll take you home."

She'd suddenly felt unwelcome and her back
stiffened with pride. "I didn't come here to be an
inconvenience. I can find my way back on my
own."

"I know it's not easy for you, but could you
humor me just this once," he'd requested dryly.
"I'm not in the mood for one of our frays."

She hadn't wanted to fight with him, either.
She'd nodded her agreement and they'd ridden
together in silence back to the Double R. Before
they parted, she told him again how sorry she
was about his grandfather and he thanked her.
But it wasn't the same as earlier. The barrier between them was firmly in place again.

"And it's always going to be there," she muttered. "He's a Colbert and I'm a Randolph and
never the twain shall meet in a real truce." An
unexpected feeling of regret suddenly washed
over her and she found herself wondering what
it would be like if she and Joe were actually in

love and getting married. Then Sam flashed through her mind and a painful knot twisted inside her. *I've been under too much strain,* she mused dryly. *My mind is taking weird flights of fantasy.*

"You all right?" Sarah questioned from the doorway.

"I'm fine," Maggie replied.

"You going to tell me what's going on between you and Joe Colbert?" Sarah asked.

The last thing Maggie wanted to do was to explain the events of the morning to another person. "It's nothing important," she said as she rose and pulled her work gloves out of her back pocket.

Sarah frowned with displeasure at this evasion. "The Colberts don't pay simple social calls on the Randolphs."

Pausing in the act of putting the gloves on, Maggie gave the housekeeper a hug. "I love you dearly, but I don't want to talk about it," she said. Then before Sarah could ask any more questions, she strode quickly out of the study.

Chester Jakes met her halfway between the house and the corral. "Just heard Joe was up at the house," he said in a protective voice.

"Thought I should come up and make certain he didn't cause any trouble."

"He didn't and he's gone," she replied. Ahead of her she saw Chester's horse being led away by one of the hands. There was foam on its neck indicating a hard ride. Obviously the cowboy who'd been working with her on the corral gate had gone to find Chester and Chester had wasted no time in getting back to the house. *No one in this county takes a meeting between a Colbert and a Randolph lightly,* she mused wearily. She knew Chester would mention it to his wife when he went home for lunch, and by midafternoon everyone within a hundred-mile radius would know Joe had been to see Frank. *Well at least they won't know why,* Maggie comforted herself. *And it's over and done with.* Keeping this thought firmly in mind, she returned to helping repair the gate.

By the time noon rolled around, she had devised several ploys to keep her grandfather satisfied for the next couple of months. Walking back to the house, she again felt she had the situation well in hand. She was even smiling when she entered the kitchen.

Hearing the door, Sarah set the knife she was using to slice tomatoes down with a clatter and turned to face Maggie. "I'd like to know why you didn't tell me yourself that there was going to be a wedding here next week," she demanded, anger and hurt sharp in her voice. "I've raised you and loved you as if you were my own daughter and when I asked you this morning what was going on, you told me 'nothing important.' Then your grandfather calls me in and tells me to cancel his lunch with Stu Gibson and to start deciding what's the best way to arrange the living room for a wedding because you and Joe are getting married." Sarah paused to gasp for breath, then finished curtly, "I didn't even have an inkling that the two of you were seeing each other."

Maggie stood frozen. Her grandfather had said he was going to take a nap. She hadn't even considered the possibility that he would take it upon himself to tell Sarah about the fictitious engagement. She'd been naive enough to believe that he would allow her and Joe to decide when and who to tell. And she certainly hadn't expected him to start making plans without con-

sulting her. How could she have been so stupid?
She should never have left his bedside.

Today has been one shock after another, she
reasoned defensively, *and I'm not thinking
straight.* For a moment she toyed with the idea of
telling Sarah the truth but the woman had her
shortcomings and not being able to keep a secret
from Frank was a very large one. "I didn't tell
you about Joe and me because I was afraid you
would disapprove," she lied. "And I didn't
mention the wedding because Joe and I haven't
actually set a date."

"Well, your grandfather has. Next Thursday,
to be exact," Sarah informed her. Then obviously somewhat appeased by Maggie's explanation, her anger faded as she continued in awed
tones, "I still can't believe this is happening. I've
always thought you should marry again but I
never pictured you and Joe Colbert together."
Flushing as if she might have said something
wrong, Sarah added quickly, "But I have to admit that the two of you do make a fine looking
couple, and it's time this feuding came to an
end."

Maggie barely heard what Sarah was saying as
the word Thursday echoed in her mind. "Hold

off on doing anything about the wedding," she said. "Joe and I want to pick our own date and there's a lot of planning I want to do."

Crossing the room, Sarah took Maggie's hand in hers. "I know Frank might be being a bit pushy," she said in a reasoning voice, "but he wants to see you married before..." Sarah stopped, unable to finish the sentence.

"I know," Maggie said soothingly, searching for excuses to postpone the wedding. "But there's Joe's family to be considered. They'll want to attend and I'm not certain they can make it as soon as next week. Now that his father is in the state legislature, his schedule is really full."

Sarah's face again showed concern. "How is his family taking the news?" Then as a thought flashed into her mind, she asked tersely, "or did they already know about the two of you?"

"No. They'll be just as surprised by the news of a wedding as you and Gramps were," she answered honestly. Then hoping to stem the tide of news from going further than this kitchen, she said, "And I don't want them to find out before Joe and I have a chance to tell them. This is very important. I want your word that you won't tell a soul." A sudden wave of fear shook Maggie.

"You haven't already told someone else, have you?"

"No, I haven't," Sarah replied, disappointed that she wasn't going to be allowed to spread the news quickly. "And I won't. But it's going to be a strain. Just imagine. A Colbert and a Randolph getting married. I never thought I'd see the day."

"Neither did I," Maggie muttered under her breath. Aloud, she said, "I need to talk to Gramps."

"I'll bring your lunch up on a tray," Sarah said. "You can eat while you talk."

The panic she was trying to control caused Maggie's stomach to rebel at the mention of food. "Don't bother." Then, knowing that Sarah would nag if she didn't give her a good reason for not eating, she added, "I'm hoping to wear my grandmother's wedding gown, which means I have to start dieting today."

"That will be lovely." Sarah smiled brightly with anticipation. "But I don't think you're going to have to diet to fit into it. I'll get it out this afternoon and you can try it on this evening. We might have to take a tuck in at the waist and let a little out at the bust. But other than that, I'll bet it fits just fine."

"I still want to skip lunch today, just to be on the safe side," Maggie insisted, then left the kitchen before Sarah could argue. Groaning inwardly she wished she had come up with another excuse. She was in no mood to humor Sarah by trying on a wedding dress when she had no intention of ever walking down an aisle in it.

Upstairs, she was greeted by Jane. "I'm so happy for you." The nurse beamed. But behind Jane's congratulatory smile, Maggie saw the curiosity and disbelief. "I know how worried your grandfather has been about you being left all alone in the world," Jane continued. "Of course this wedding is going to come as quite a shock to a lot of people."

Joe and me included, Maggie thought. On the way upstairs, her mind had cleared enough to figure out how to handle Sarah and it would work with Jane. She'd simply tell them this evening that she and Joe had a terrible fight and the wedding was off. Then she'd beg them to keep this from her grandfather so he wouldn't get upset. It would be taking a big chance to trust Sarah, but she had to. News of this fictitious engagement had to stay within the confines of this house. As embarrassing as it would be, she would even tell them the whole truth if necessary. Aloud, she said, "Joe's family still doesn't know and we want them to find out from us. I hope you'll keep our engagement in confidence until we can tell them." Then the wave of fear washed over her again. "You haven't told anyone else yet, have you?"

"No, I haven't and, of course, I won't until you want me to," Jane agreed, a gleam in her eyes suggesting that she wished she could be there when the Colberts found out.

"Thanks," Maggie said, breathing a sigh of relief. Now that she had Sarah and Jane under control, it was time to deal with her grandfather. Entering his room she found him propped up in a sitting position looking more alive than he had in months. But it was the phone on his lap that held her attention. Her face paled and her mouth formed a grim line.

"Now don't begrudge an old man his final wish," he said with a broad grin. "I can tell by the look on your face that Sarah has told you I've set the date for your wedding. I know it's short notice but I don't have much longer in this world and I want to see you married before my time comes.''

"I understand how you feel, but weddings take time to arrange, and I can't speak for Joe." Maggie felt as if she were grabbing at straws. A few moments ago she thought she had this situation in hand but the phone on her grandfather's lap unnerved her. Who had he been calling now? "I know Joe wants his parents to be present and his father is a very busy man. I really need more time."

"Time is something I don't have," Frank reminded her again grimly. Then his smile returned. "I spoke to Joe just a few minutes ago. He says Thursday is fine with him."

How could Joe have agreed? Maggie wished she had his neck between her hands so that she could strangle him.

"And I've arranged for Doc Jones to do your blood test when he comes by to see me tomorrow," Frank continued. "Then he'll stop by Joe's place and do his. After that, all you two have to do is get the license and we're set. I hope you don't mind, but it's going to have to be a small wedding—just family. And it's going to have to be here . . . Doc Jones's orders. I set the time with Reverend Smith for four o'clock. You can decorate the living room with flowers and Sarah will have a real special dinner for everyone afterward."

Maggie opened her mouth to protest but her grandfather raised his hand to silence her. "I've already spoken with Joe about these arrangements and he says they're all fine with him."

Maggie felt as if the walls were closing in on her. "I need to talk to Joe," she said tightly. "We haven't discussed who is going to be best man or maid of honor. There are a lot of details we need to work out." Giving her grandfather a quick kiss, she practically flew out of the room and out of the house. Climbing into her car she again wished she could get her hands around Joe Colbert's neck. How could he blithely agree to everything?

To her relief, no one at the White Stallion Ranch seemed to know anything about the wedding. Helen Davis, Joe's housekeeper, looked surprised to see Maggie at their door. As she led her toward Joe's study to wait for him, Helen kept glancing at Maggie as if she couldn't quite believe a Randolph was setting foot in the Colbert house. There was no overt hostility in the housekeeper's manner, but there was a certain suspicious concern and a definite air of protectiveness toward Joe. After all, Helen had been housekeeper at the Colbert ranch for nearly as long as Sarah had been at the Double R.

"If you'll wait here, I'll send one of the hands to the stables to fetch Joe," Helen said formally, opening the study door and stepping aside to allow Maggie to enter. But as she started to leave, she paused and added with sincerity, "I am sorry to hear about your grandfather being so ill."

"Thank you," Maggie replied. The kind words helped her feel less like she was in enemy territory, but not a whole lot less.

Left alone, Maggie glanced around the study. It had an unmistakable masculine feel to it. This was definitely Joe's lair. Too taut to sit, she paced. How could things have gotten so far out of hand in a single morning? Hearing booted feet coming down the hall, she stiffened and turned toward the door.

"I was wondering if you would show up," Joe said, entering and closing the door behind him.

Holding herself under tight control, Maggie glared at him. "How could you agree to a wedding date?"

"And a blood test," he added coolly.

"And a blood test," she repeated through clenched teeth.

Crossing the room to stand in front of her, he regarded her dryly. "I considered telling him the truth. But then I thought of Stu Gibson and my heart went out to the man. He's used to having a woman around who's gentle and docile, who would wait on him hand and foot, obey his every wish and never, never talk back. You would have been a tremendous shock to him."

Maggie scowled as a cynical smile played at the corners of Joe's mouth. "This is not a joking matter!"

The smile disappeared. "No it's not," he agreed.

"You could have refused to set a positive date. You could have told him you didn't think we could put a wedding together that fast. You could have told him to talk to me about it," she snapped.

"You're right." His jaw tightened with purpose. "But I didn't. After I left you this morning, I had some time to think about this matter and I came to the conclusion that a marriage between the two of us is a good idea."

Maggie stared at him in shock. "You decided what?"

"I decided we would make a great couple," he answered dryly.

Maggie shook her head in total disbelief. "You can't be serious."

"I am very serious," he assured her. "You lied to your grandfather. If he finds out the truth there's no telling what he'll do. The vindictiveness of the Randolph mind has always stunned me."

"We're no more vindictive than the Colberts," she shot back at him.

Ignoring her remark, Joe continued in a businesslike tone, "At the very least you'll be coerced into marrying Stu Gibson. And like I said, I can't, in good conscience, let such a disaster befall the man."

"You are just full of compliments," she said, seethingly.

The hint of a smile appeared on his face, then disappeared as his expression again became deadly serious. "Therefore, I have decided to marry you myself. We'll stay married until your grandfather dies and a reasonable period of mourning has passed, then we'll get a divorce and you will have your ranch."

Maggie studied him coldly. "You're going to make the ultimate sacrifice—marry me to save my ranch for me and to save Stu Gibson from a fate worse than death—out of the goodness of your Colbert heart? I don't buy that for one minute."

He shrugged a shoulder nonchalantly. "There would be a little something in it for me."

The suspicion in Maggie's eyes doubled. "What 'little something'?"

"Wild Horse Canyon. After the divorce, you'll sell it to me at a reasonable price." He regarded her levelly. "It's a fair deal, Maggie. We both get what we want and nobody gets hurt."

She had to admit it was an equitable solution to a difficult problem. But there was one thing they had to get straight before she could agree. "It would be a marriage in name only."

Challenge flickered in Joe's eyes. "I know when a woman is responding, Maggie, and you practically melted in my arms when I kissed you. It's time you stopped living with a ghost. You need a flesh-and-blood man."

He moved toward her. She knew he intended to prove his point by kissing her again. Sam Hagan's image came strongly into her mind. "No!" she said curtly, taking a step back to keep the distance between them.

Coming to a halt, Joe regarded her grimly. "For pete's sake, Maggie, you were still a teenager when Sam Hagan died. He wouldn't expect you to live the rest of your life like a nun just to honor his memory."

Her whole body tensed. "It's my choice. Our marriage will be in name only or it won't happen."

For a long moment he regarded her in silence, then drawing a harsh breath, he said, "If that's the way you want it, it's fine with me."

"A Randolph's handshake is as good as a signed contract," she said stiffly. "I've heard the same is true for a Colbert."

"It's true," he affirmed.

"Then will you shake on this agreement?"

In answer, Joe held out his hand. She wiped the perspiration from her palm onto her jeans, then extended her hand to meet his. She'd expected the handshake to feel like any business handshake but as his large, work-callused hand engulfed hers, a warmth spread up her arm and trailed through her whole body. Startled again by her strong reaction to his touch, she trembled involuntarily.

The frown on his face deepened. "You don't have to be afraid of me."

"I'm not," she replied, trying to steel her body against any further display of the disquieting effect he had on her. It wasn't easy. When he called Helen in to inform her about the wedding, he placed a possessive arm around Maggie's shoulders. In spite of her desire to feel nothing, she was filled with a mixture of emotions. Again there was the warmth but there was also fear. She was very aware of his strength. She knew she wasn't strong enough to fight him off if he should decide to ignore the terms of their bargain. Trying to look like a happy fiancée instead of a frightened rabbit, she kept a plastic smile on her face while she reassured herself that Joe's handshake was his word of honor and he wouldn't go against it.

Helen was speechless for a moment as if she needed time for the words to sink in. Then, watching Joe dubiously, she said, "I've always thought you needed a wife." When he responded with a warm smile, she turned her attention to Maggie. "I hope you realize what a good man you have here."

"I do," Maggie lied, wondering how she could sound so calm when she was shaking like a leaf inside.

This assurance seemed to be what Helen needed. "Then you have my best wishes." Turning back to Joe, she added, "It's about time you got married."

"Yes, ma'am," he replied with a playful wink. Then his manner became businesslike. "You should call Sarah Martin and offer to help with the reception. And since there is very little time, I want you to show Maggie around the house right now. She'll have to decide how she wants the drawers and closets in my bedroom rearranged to hold her things."

The words "in my bedroom" echoed through Maggie's mind. He intended for them to share a bedroom! Obviously his handshake had meant nothing! She started to pull away from him but Joe's hold on her tightened.

He glanced down at her, his eyes warning her to behave.

Her own eyes held ice. She stopped her bid for freedom because she didn't want to cause a scene in front of Helen. But as soon as they were alone, she planned to tell him what she thought of his deviousness and what he could do with his plan for them to share a bedroom.

Turning his attention back to Helen, Joe said, "Would you wait for Maggie in the hall? I'd like a little privacy to say goodbye to my fiancée."

Smiling knowingly, Helen left the room.

Maggie waited until the housekeeper had closed the door behind her, then jerked free of Joe's hold. Turning she faced him hostilely. "You agreed to a marriage in name only," she hissed, keeping her voice low.

Joe regarded her coolly. "People around here expect newly married couples to share the same bedroom and the same bed. You wouldn't want to go to all this trouble and then have your grandfather suspect we weren't being honest with him, would you?"

"Same bed?" she choked out, ready to fight this with every ounce of strength she had.

"You have my word I won't touch you against your will."

Maggie read the angry promise in his eyes. She should have been relieved, but instead she felt as if she had been insulted, as if he didn't find her attractive enough to warrant any effort toward intimacy. *But that's exactly what I want,* she chided herself curtly. This whole day has been insane and it's causing my reactions to be irrational, she reasoned. Drawing a steadying breath, she faced him. "Just make certain you keep that promise." Without waiting for a response, she left the room to join Helen in the hall.

"I hope you won't be offended if I say I'm a bit surprised," the housekeeper said as she took Maggie on a quick tour of the downstairs.

"We were keeping it a secret from my grandfather because we didn't want to upset him," Maggie explained. "But he wants me married before he dies. He was even going to pick out a husband for me so I had to tell him about Joe. He took it much better than I thought he would." This last statement was certainly true, Maggie mused, still wondering how such a small lie could have gotten her into such a big mess.

"Well, for your sake and Joe's, I'm glad." Pausing halfway up the stairs, Helen turned to face Maggie. "I've always been loyal to the Colberts but I don't really believe in feuding. I'm glad it's over."

"Me, too," Maggie managed to say, wondering how Helen would feel toward the Randolphs when the marriage ended as abruptly as it had begun.

Entering Joe's bedroom, Maggie felt a cold sweat break out on the palms of her hands. While the rest of the house had a strong masculine feel to it, it also looked comfortable and homey. But this room intimidated her. *It's all in your mind,* she chided herself angrily. Glancing toward the bed, she breathed a small sigh of relief. It was king-size. There would be plenty of room for her and Joe to lie apart.

"I can move all of Joe's things into one closet and you can have the other all to yourself," Helen said as she opened the closet doors and scanned the contents.

Maggie smiled woodenly and nodded.

"And I can clear out half the chest of drawers for you," Helen continued, moving to the bureau. The ring of the phone caught her in mid-stride. Excusing herself, she left to answer it.

Alone in the room, Maggie looked around slowly. As her eyes traveled over the bedside table, they narrowed. There was an old faded blue ribbon tied around the base of the lamp. Like a moth drawn to a flame, she moved toward it. It couldn't be, she told herself. But it was. Reaching the table, she stared down at the worn piece of satin. She knew as surely as she knew her name that the ribbon had been hers. She'd been wearing it on the day all those years ago when Joe kissed her. Being childishly romantic, she'd given it to him so he would look at it and think of her when they were apart. "Why would he keep it?" she wondered aloud, frowning in confusion.

"I keep it to remind myself that the Colberts and the Randolphs can never be anything at heart but enemies."

Startled, she turned to find Joe standing a couple of feet away from her. Her attention had been so riveted on the ribbon, she hadn't heard him enter. There was a coldness in his gaze as it traveled from her to the ribbon and back again.

"I suppose you're right," she admitted, recalling the bitterness of their parting so many years ago.

Joe shrugged as if to say "what is, is," and the

coldness in his eyes faded to indifference. "Helen asked me to tell you she's on the phone with Sarah. They're discussing food and Sarah needs to ask you something about a wedding gown." His message delivered, he turned away from her and left the room.

Maggie's gaze traveled to the bed. A marriage of enemies. That suited her just fine.

Chapter Three

The next few days passed nervously for Maggie while the preparations for the wedding moved along quickly. She wanted Sarah to be her maid of honor, which meant finding someone else to prepare dinner and serve it. At first, Sarah was frantic but Helen volunteered for the job and that crisis was averted.

The most embarrassing incident during the week was when Frank called Joe over to sign the prenuptial agreement. He made it clear that while he was willing to let Maggie follow her heart, he still didn't completely trust Joe.

"You mistreat my granddaughter and you'll have me to answer to," Frank warned Joe. "If I'm already dead, then I promise you, my ghost will come back to haunt you."

"Gramps, really," Maggie admonished with an angry scowl.

But Joe was not flustered. "I'll remember that," he said with no show of irritation.

Invitations to the wedding were issued by phone rather than by mail, and only very close friends and family were invited.

Joe handled contacting his family. It took some courage but Maggie finally made herself ask him how they were taking the news of the marriage.

"They've accepted it agreeably," he assured her.

"I find it hard to believe your father wouldn't raise some objections," she persisted, wanting to have some warning if there was the possibility of a brawl at the wedding.

"My father's great love is politics. He will not jeopardize his present office or any future aspirations by maintaining a feud that could be used against him by his opponents. In fact, he's very happy about this marriage," Joe informed her firmly.

On the surface, Maggie accepted this explanation but deep down inside she was still worried. By the day of the wedding her nerves were on a razor's edge.

From her bedroom window, she watched the Colberts arrive. Both the Double R and the White Stallion ranches were a long, hot drive from the nearest town so they'd flown into San Angelo and rented a helicopter to bring them the rest of the way to the ranch. Joe owned a small helicopter, which he used for quick inspections of his ranch and for emergency trips into town, but it was too small to carry his parents, his brother and his brother's family from San Angelo to the ranch in just one trip.

As the dust settled and everyone disembarked, Maggie noted that they looked a little uneasy but not hostile. Still, she was glad they would be returning to Houston as soon as the wedding was over. Because of her grandfather's illness, she and Joe would not be going on a honeymoon and she didn't relish spending her first night at the White Stallion Ranch with Joe and his entire family.

As soon as everyone was seated in the living room, Sarah came to get Maggie. Frank was too weak to walk his granddaughter down the aisle. Instead, he sat in a wheelchair and waited for her beside Joe and the preacher.

Standing alone in the hall, Maggie nervously watched Sarah enter the living room walking in step to the music. Then the pianist struck a loud chord and the bridal march filled the air. As she reached the entrance to the living room, the urge to bolt grew strong. Then Joe was coming toward her. He looked handsome in his dark blue suit and he was smiling. But the smile didn't reach those brown eyes of his. They warned her to behave.

Reaching her, he tucked her arm through his and escorted her the rest of the way.

The ceremony was a blur to Maggie. Finally Reverend Smith pronounced them husband and wife and Joe lifted her veil for the traditional kiss. "Are you going to faint, Maggie?" he asked in a concerned whisper when he saw her face.

"I hope not," she replied shakily.

"It'll be all right," he assured her gruffly. "Trust me." Then he kissed her gently.

It was a quick, easy kiss but Maggie felt her blood suddenly rushing through her veins. *Well at least I won't faint,* she told herself, unnerved again by the strong physical reactions she had toward this man.

During the dinner following the wedding, a jovial atmosphere prevailed—at least on the surface. Joe's father toasted the bride and groom while Joe's mother gave Maggie a welcome-to-the-Colbert-clan hug. But behind the good wishes, Maggie sensed tension and doubt. She suspected the majority of the guests were betting the marriage wouldn't last. *And they'll be proved right,* she mused tiredly, her plastic smile beginning to feel brittle.

Finally they cut the cake and Maggie tossed her bouquet. Drawing a deep sigh of relief, she allowed Joe to escort her to his waiting car.

But the relief was short-lived. As soon as she had waved her goodbyes and the car began to pull away, a shiver of apprehension shook her. Legally she was Joe's wife. What if he chose to ignore their agreement? What if he decided to exercise his husbandly rights? Curtly she reminded herself that they had shaken on the deal and the one thing she knew for certain about a

Colbert was that his handshake was his bond. Fighting back an attack of nerves, she concentrated on the sunset in the distance.

"You looked very pretty today," Joe said, breaking the silence between them.

"You looked pretty good yourself," she replied, trying to sound casual.

"Thanks." He glanced toward her and the smile on his face became an impatient frown. "You look like Red Riding-Hood expecting the big bad wolf to jump out at her at any minute. I gave you my word I wouldn't demand any intimacy from you."

He was telling her what she wanted to hear, so why did it feel as if it were an insult? *He's not interested in me as a woman, and that's the way I want it,* she affirmed tightly. Still the sting of his words refused to vanish entirely. *I'm just tired,* she told herself.

When they arrived at the house, Joe insisted on carrying her over the threshold. "More than any other couple I know, we need good luck to carry this off," he said, scooping her up in his arms.

"You're right," she agreed, deciding that arguing would be silly. But as he lifted her in his arms, she was beset by a confusion of emotions. At first, warmth spread through her and a stirring of desire began to grow within her. Then the memories of Sam Hagan assailed her and coldness filled her. Suddenly she was aware only of Joe's strength. Again it crossed her mind that physically she was no match for him.

"I noticed you didn't eat much at dinner. Why don't you go change into something more comfortable and we'll raid the refrigerator," he suggested, setting her down in the entrance hall. "I told Helen to stock it with sandwich fixings in case we were hungry."

"I suppose Helen will be getting back late," Maggie muttered uneasily.

"Helen won't be back until late tomorrow," he informed her. "She knew we couldn't go on a honeymoon because your grandfather is so ill and she thought we'd like our first night together alone. So, when she's done at the Double R, she's going to her sister's to spend the night."

A cold sweat broke out on Maggie's brow. "She's not coming back tonight?"

Annoyance mingled with impatience on Joe's face. "It was her decision. I couldn't argue with

her. It would have looked suspicious. New-
lyweds usually want their privacy."

He made her feel like a foolish child. *That's
because you're acting like one,* she chided herself. *How many times does he have to tell you he
isn't interested in you before you believe him?*
"It's been a long day," she said apologetically.
"I'm feeling a little—make that a lot—high-
strung and I'm sorry." Needing some time alone,
she added, "I think I will change and I am hungry. I'll meet you in the kitchen in a few minutes."

Upstairs in his room that was now "their"
bedroom, a fresh wave of nerves washed over
her. The bed looked smaller than she remembered. *Stop being ridiculous!* she scolded herself. *He's assured you a hundred times that
you're safe from his advances.*

Furious with herself for feeling like a frightened schoolgirl, she unfastened the buttons of
the wedding dress. As she hung the lovely, old-
fashioned lace gown in the closet, a bitter smile
came to her face. Vividly she recalled one summer afternoon when she was about eight. She
and her mother were cleaning closets and they
paused to look at the wedding dress. "When you

walk down the aisle in this gown," her mother had said with a soft, happy smile, "I want that day to be the beginning of a lifetime of happiness for you just as it was for your grandmother and for me."

Gently Maggie touched the lace sleeve. She hadn't worn the dress when she and Sam Hagan married. They'd eloped. Later she was glad the tradition of the dress hadn't been tainted by a marriage that left her a widow after less than ten months. Cynically she wondered if a marriage that wasn't really a marriage counted.

"I thought you were coming down to get something to eat," Joe said from the doorway.

Whirling around, she saw his eyes rake over her in a purely masculine inspection. Their color darkened, indicating that he liked what he saw. For a split second her body warmed beneath his approval. Then a cold sweat broke out on her brow once more. Whirling back around, she grabbed a shirt from the closet to cover herself.

When she turned around again, she found him watching her speculatively.

"You're not as immune to me as you want me to believe," he said levelly. "I saw the way the green of your eyes flickered just now, and when

I've kissed you, I've felt your body threaten to ignite in my hands."

Her strong instinct for self-protection demanded she deny his allegations, even if they were true. "I—"

"And I would be lying if I said I don't find you desirable," he continued, cutting her denial short. "I'm a man and you're a very attractive woman. But I made you a promise, Maggie, and I'll abide by it."

Maggie's chin trembled. She wanted to tell him she felt nothing for him but indifference. Instead she stood frozen and speechless.

"I'm going to change into a pair of jeans," he said, breaking the silence between them. Reaching his closet in four long strides, he pulled out the clothing he wanted. Without glancing at her as he walked back toward the door, he added over his shoulder, "I'll change in the guest room and meet you downstairs."

Maggie watched him leave and close the door behind him. Continuing to stand rigid, she listened to his footsteps as he crossed the hall and entered the guest room. She knew she had behaved badly. She should have told him to go ahead and change in here. Once Helen was back in the house, he couldn't go off to the guest room every time he needed to change clothes. *I just need a little time to adjust,* she defended herself shakily. Maggie stared at the pale face in the mirror. *I have my reasons for being the way I am and I can't change instantly.* Promising herself she would try to keep a level head on her shoulders, she changed into a pair of jeans and the shirt she'd pulled from the closet, then went down to the kitchen.

Joe was already there. "Helen's a romantic," he said with an edge of cynicism, nodding toward a platter of small, fancy sandwiches and a chilled bottle of champagne the housekeeper had left for them.

Maggie forced a smile. "That was very nice of her." Accepting the glass of sparkling wine he handed her, she seated herself at the table. For the hundredth time she assured herself she had nothing to fear from him. But as hard as she tried, she couldn't stop thinking that they had a long night ahead of them and they were totally alone.

Ignore him, she ordered herself. *Just pretend he isn't here.* Determined to present a calm front, she picked up one of the sandwiches and took a bite of it.

However, Joe was not an easy man to ignore. In fact, he was an impossible man to ignore. While she sat, he chose to stand, leaning against the counter in a casual pose. Even relaxed, there was a sense of animal strength about him. She couldn't stop him if he decided to demand his conjugal rights.

But he isn't going to, she reminded herself firmly. *He promised.*

Still her nerves remained taut. She couldn't forget the way his eyes had darkened as they traveled over her half-dressed body or his admission that he found her desirable. The silence in the kitchen didn't help either. It seemed to get heavier with each passing moment. *Think of something to say,* she ordered herself. His work seemed like a safe topic. "I understand you've developed quite a reputation as a breeder." A sudden flush spread from her neck to her face. "Horse breeder," she amended quickly.

A hint of amusement glistened in his eyes, then they became unreadable as he said, "It's all a matter of choosing your stock carefully."

Maggie had the distinct feeling he wasn't talking entirely about horses. *You're just overly sensitive,* she told herself. *Now keep the conversation going; it's better than the silence.* "I hear you have some Appaloosa and you're thinking of looking into getting some good Arabian stock."

"You heard right." Hooking his thumbs through the belt loops on his jeans, he continued in a slow drawl, "But it's my quarter horses I concentrate on the most. A cowboy needs a strong horse with staying power. I've been experimenting with breeding them with wild mustangs. I figure it could be a good mix. The quarter horses are getting a little too tame for me. I like an animal with fight in its blood."

Horse breeding was definitely a bad topic, Maggie decided. Joe hadn't said anything improper or pushy, but the atmosphere in the kitchen felt charged. Hoping it would relax her, she gulped down the glass of champagne. That was an even worse mistake. The alcohol hit her system almost immediately and weakened the hold she had on the fears nagging at her. An uncontrollable wave of nausea assailed her. Running from the kitchen, she took the stairs two at a time in her desperate flight to the bathroom. When she came out a few minutes later, she found Joe leaning against the bedroom wall, waiting for her.

"You all right?" he asked gruffly.

"I think I have a touch of the flu," she lied.

"Looked like an attack of pure panic to me," he said with the angry impatience she was beginning to know so well.

Pride demanded that she refute him. "I'm just very tired, and I shouldn't have drank the champagne so fast."

The look on his face said he wasn't buying this explanation. "I've already told you several times, you don't have to be afraid of me. I promise I won't make any demands on you." A strong note of sarcasm entered his voice as he added, "If you want to keep yourself as a sacred shrine to your late husband, that's your right. I wouldn't dream of violating holy ground." Without waiting for a response, he stalked out of the room, slamming the door behind him.

"Well, you should feel safe now," she muttered to herself. "He's made it perfectly clear he wouldn't touch you with a ten foot pole!"

Maggie's chin tightened. "And that's the way I want it," she stated firmly.

Exhausted, she stared at the bed. At least she couldn't make a fool of herself while she was sleeping, she reasoned.

She showered, hoping to relax her taut muscles, then pulled out a modest cotton nightgown and put it on. Standing hesitantly at the foot of the bed, she wondered what side Joe normally slept on. The bedside table on the left held both the phone and the radio. Logically that would be the side he preferred. The problem was, it was also the side she usually slept on. "I'll get used to the other side." Mentally she commanded herself to stay on her side of the bed. Climbing under the covers, she fidgeted, turning first on her side, then her back, then her stomach, then her other side, then back to her original position, trying to get comfortable. She was afraid she would never be able to relax and get to sleep, but the exhaustion of the long day and the constant strain on her nerves proved her wrong. After only a few more minutes of tossing and turning, she was lost in the blissful escape of sleep. But even that peace didn't last. Nightmares came to haunt her.

* * *

The next morning Maggie awoke slowly and groggily. With her eyes still closed, she became aware that her cheek was resting against something warm and hard. Stretching lazily, her whole body came up against a warm barrier. But she didn't mind. There was something very comforting about it. Still half asleep, she snuggled closer. Something tickled her nose. She reached up to scratch it and felt crisp, curly hair beneath her palm. Her eyes popped open.

She was lying with her head on a very male chest, with her body snuggled along the length of a very masculine form. Lifting her head, she followed the line of the body upward until she found herself staring into Joe's dark gaze. His arm curved around her, holding her gently and for a moment a need stirred within her, then her stomach knotted. "Let go of me," she stammered.

Immediately she was freed and like a frightened animal, she scurried out of the bed. She could feel him watching her as she pulled on her robe. Embarrassment intertwined with fear until she wasn't certain which was stronger. What she *was* certain of was that she had to get away. She fled the room and went downstairs.

As she stood on the patio watching the sun rise, trying to steady her jumbled nerves, she heard him approach. She turned to face him and her breath locked in her lungs. He was wearing only his jeans and for the first time, she had a full view of his upper torso. As her eyes traveled from his hard, flat abdomen to his chest, then up to his unshaven face and rumpled hair, she felt his virility as if it were a physical force. Again the beginnings of desire stirred within her, then Sam Hagan's image filled her mind and the coldness returned.

"I wasn't making a play for you," he said gruffly. "When I came to bed last night you were tossing and turning. Seemed like you were having one hell of a nightmare. I tried to wake you, but I couldn't. Then I tried talking to you. When I told you everything would be all right, you curled up with your head on my shoulder and settled down so I just let you stay there. I figured it was the only way I was going to get any rest. I sure couldn't sleep with you fighting your way through the night."

Raking a hand through her hair, Maggie fought back a flush of embarrassment. She'd been wrong. Even asleep she managed to make a fool of herself. "I'm sorry for overreacting," she said stiffly.

Shoving his hands into the pockets of his jeans, Joe studied her darkly. "You can trust me, Maggie. A man would be a fool to try to compete with the hallowed memory of your short but blissful marriage, and I don't like to think of myself as a fool. If you want to live with a ghost, that's your business. The only thing I want is for us to make your grandfather believe we're happily married, and that means convincing everyone else, too." Turning on his heels, he stalked back into the house.

Maggie drew a short breath. Joe was right about one thing, they did need to convince the populace their marriage was working. "Let the show begin," she commanded herself.

Going upstairs, she went into the bedroom. The door of the adjoining bathroom was open and Joe stood in front of the mirror shaving. Feeling she was invading his privacy, she started to leave. Then, reminding herself that she was supposed to be acting like a real wife, she forced herself to approach the open doorway. "Do you want pancakes or eggs with your bacon?" she asked, coming to a halt on the threshold.

Pausing, Joe studied her in the mirror. "You really don't have to go to any trouble for me," he said. "I can fix something for myself."

"It's a wife's duty to see that her husband has a good breakfast before he goes off to work," she replied. When she saw the skepticism in his eyes, she added, "You don't have to worry. I can cook."

"Pancakes, then," he said.

"Pancakes it is." Normally she would have dressed before going back to the kitchen but she wasn't ready to act that married.

Breakfast went reasonably well. She managed not to burn anything and Joe complimented her on the food. More importantly, they were able to carry on a polite conversation without it ending in a hostile exchange or with her fleeing the room in a panic. Of course they kept their talk strictly to what their plans for the day would be.

Joe had work to do around the ranch and Maggie wanted to go visit her grandfather.

After Joe left, Maggie cleaned up the kitchen, then changed into some riding clothes. Leaving the house, she walked toward the barns. Ahead of her in a corral with several other horses, she saw Gray Dawn, her horse. The mare seemed right at home. "I'm glad one of us is adjusting easily," she noted.

"Morning, Mrs. Colbert," a young ranch hand greeted her as she reached the corral. "You want your horse saddled?"

"Yes, thanks," she replied, quickly recovering from the shock of being addressed by her married name. For the first time it dawned on her that legally she was a Colbert. After all these years of considering Colbert a dirty word, she *was* one. A self-mocking smile crossed her face. Hearing the sound of horses hooves behind her, she turned to see Joe approaching.

"Thought I'd ride over to the Double R with you," he said, bringing his horse to a halt beside her. "A couple of the hands say they've seen fresh mountain lion tracks." For a moment Maggie could have sworn she saw a protectiveness in his eyes. But it was gone as he added, "Folks around here would expect me to make certain my new wife is kept safe."

Balking at the idea that he saw this as a baby-sitting chore, she frowned. "I know how to take care of myself. I've ridden these ranges hundreds of times when a mountain lion was on the prowl."

"I know," he conceded. Then in a low, but firm voice, he said, "But you weren't married to me then. Now you are and you're my responsibility."

Maggie was about to challenge this assumption when the young ranch hand came back with her horse. Not wanting to create a scene, she thanked him, mounted Gray Dawn and rode off with Joe by her side.

But later in her grandfather's room, she wished she had insisted that Joe stay home. They had arrived at the Double R to discover that Frank was in one of his more cantankerous moods.

"He's been wanting me to call you all morning," Sarah told Maggie. Her cheeks flushed scarlet in apology as she glanced at Joe. "He's suddenly decided to worry that he's pushed you into a marriage you'll regret."

It's a little late for him to be thinking about that, Maggie thought acidly. Aloud, she said, "He has nothing to worry about."

Sarah gave Joe a bright smile. "That's exactly what I told him."

Knowing how difficult her grandfather could be, Maggie was about to suggest that Joe remain downstairs while she went to talk to him, but as if he could read her mind, Joe said, "We'd better go upstairs and reassure him." Taking her by the arm, he started toward her grandfather's room.

Becoming more anxious with each step about what Frank Randolph might say, Maggie came to an abrupt halt outside his bedroom door. "I really think I should see him alone," she said tightly.

"I don't think so," Joe replied. "I want to know what's on his mind."

The firm set of his jaw told her that arguing would be useless, so bracing herself for whatever was going to happen, she opened the door.

"'Bout time you stopped by to see how I was doing," Frank growled from his bed. "Been worrying about you all morning, girl." Scowling at Joe, he asked curtly, "You been treating my granddaughter right?"

"Right as rain," Joe replied in an easy drawl.

Frank didn't look convinced. Turning back to Maggie he said, "Been thinking I'd better stick around awhile just to make certain this Colbert don't revert to kind."

Joe was standing beside Maggie and she felt him tense. "The Colberts aren't any better or worse than the Randolphs," she heard herself saying. "Both families are as stubborn as mules and because of that we've had our differences. But that's in the past." Maggie caught the momentary glint of surprise in Joe's eyes before they became masked. But he wasn't half as surprised as she was by her defense of his family.

Frank scowled skeptically. "For your sake, I hope you're right."

"I am," she assured him. Then before her grandfather could say anything else offensive about the Colberts, she said, "And now I think it's time you got some rest. I'll come back tomorrow."

But Frank always did insist on having the final word. "You can leave your husband at home," he called out as Maggie headed for the door.

Out in the hall, she turned to Joe apologetically. "I'm sorry he was so rude."

Joe studied her face as if trying to read what was going on in her mind. "Did you really mean what you said in there? You don't consider my family to be basically mean and evil?"

Maggie thought for a moment, then answered honestly. "No, I don't, not really. I've never heard of any of you doing anything cruel. The only real fighting your family has ever done has been with mine and then it's been either verbal or legal. There's never been any bloodshed." Remembering the pain the dispute over Wild Horse Canyon caused her, she added tightly, "Sometimes, it just feels like there has been."

"Yeah," Joe conceded gruffly.

Chapter Four

During the next few weeks, life grew more and more difficult for Maggie. She thought that after the wedding, she and Joe would settle into a manageable routine and the days would pass reasonably smoothly. They did settle into a routine and on the surface the days seemed to pass reasonably smoothly. But underneath, tension was building.

Her grandfather was true to his word: he had found a new will to live and was improving each and every day. "I couldn't have found a wonder drug more powerful than your marriage to a

Colbert,'' Doc Jones told Maggie. Although Maggie was happy about her grandfather's renewed health, it did put a whole new complexion on her arrangement with Joe. Their marriage, which was to have lasted only a short time, now seemed as if it would go on forever.

Joe didn't say anything or complain, but she felt the strain between them growing worse with each passing hour. For the first couple of weeks after the wedding, he'd brought her flowers almost daily and played the attentive bridegroom to the hilt. Now he avoided her whenever possible, and when they were alone together, he was brittlely polite. In public they kept up the pretense of the happily married couple, but even that was wearing thin.

Six weeks today, Maggie thought while lying in bed late one night twisting her wedding band around and around on her finger. She glanced over at the bedside table. The luminous dial on the clock told her it was a few minutes past midnight. *We were married six weeks ago, yesterday,* she corrected.

Joe should have been in bed by now, but he wasn't. She knew where he was—in his study, where he had spent every night for the past two weeks. At about four in the morning, before Helen got up, he would come up to the bedroom, shower and dress for the day.

Maggie reached a decision. "This has got to stop!" she announced to the darkness that surrounded her. Throwing the covers off, she snapped on the light and got out of bed. Now that she was in motion, she did not slow down for fear she might turn back. Grabbing her robe, she pulled it on, left the bedroom and descended the stairs. At the study door, she knocked once, then entered.

Still dressed in his work clothes, Joe was asleep on the couch. There was a small travel alarm on the coffee table. Standing over him, she hesitated. But even in sleep, the lines of strain were etched into his face and she knew this had to end. "Joe," she said, shaking him gently.

Opening his eyes, he frowned. "What do you want?"

Maggie stepped back a couple of paces as he levered himself into a sitting position and rubbed the sleep out of his eyes. "We have to talk," she said.

The frown on his face deepened. "Couldn't this wait until morning?"

His anger weakened her courage and she was tempted to say yes. But she managed a firm, "No."

He drew an impatient breath. "What is it, then?"

Folding her arms in front of her, she said levelly, "This cannot go on. While for my sake, I'm glad my grandfather's health has improved, I realize this has been an unexpected and difficult turn of events for you."

"I do *not* wish your grandfather dead," he growled, clearly indignant that she might think he would.

"I know that," she assured him quickly. Raking a hand through her hair, she continued. "But I also know you hadn't planned on my being here indefinitely. I've made your home uncomfortable for you and that's not right or fair. I feel the time has come to call an end to this marriage."

Rising from the couch, Joe paced around the room. Then, coming to a halt in front of her, he said grimly, "Your grandfather will simply insist on marrying you off to someone else. And that someone else might not be as understanding as I am."

Maggie's jaw tightened. "I can handle my grandfather."

"Like you handled him this time?" he questioned dryly.

Maggie had to admit that from the moment she'd frantically devised the plan to thwart her grandfather's attempt to marry her off, nothing had worked out as she had anticipated. But she wasn't going to compound her errors by making more. "I can't stay here. You hate having me here. You're miserable with me here."

For a long moment he regarded her in a black silence. Then he said gruffly, "I don't hate having you here and I'm not miserable. I'm frustrated." He paced across the room, putting distance between them. Then turning back to face her, he said bluntly, "I'm not made of stone, Maggie. You're a desirable woman and you're my wife but I've agreed not to touch you. That's enough to put a strain on any man."

Maggie stared at him. After their confrontation on their wedding night, he had not made a move toward her. "I thought you weren't interested in me that way," she said shakily.

"I suppose you thought all those flowers and the attention I paid you in the beginning were all for show?" he demanded.

"Yes," she replied tightly. "You always got sort of cool right afterward."

"Because you always got that frightened look in your eyes—like the one you have now, as if you're afraid I might try to seduce you and tarnish your memories," he growled. "You made it perfectly clear in a thousand unspoken and spoken ways that you don't want me near you."

Maggie spread her hands in a helpless gesture. "I am the way I am," she said. "I can't change that."

"I'm not asking you to." His jaw hardened and he squared his shoulders. "We made a deal and we're going to abide by it. Now go back to bed."

She studied the strain lines on his face. "You must really want Wild Horse Canyon badly."

"Go to bed, Maggie," he ordered in a voice that held no compromise.

She knew this situation was not good for either of them, but they had struck a deal and as long as he wanted to abide by it, she would have to, also. Her Randolph honor demanded it.

"Good night," she said tiredly and went back upstairs.

Lying in bed in the dark, she reached over and touched his pillow. She missed his being there. This admission frightened her, but it was the truth. Hot tears burned at the back of her eyes.

The next morning, she woke exhausted, her head aching. She had fought her memories of Sam Hagan all night and they'd won. But during the battle, she'd been forced to face one uncomfortable truth: she did care about Joe more than she wanted to admit. Even now the pain of their parting so many years ago was still there, buried deep in the recesses of her heart. "It's just as well the memories won," she told herself grimly, staring at the circles under her eyes in the bathroom mirror. "The last thing I need is to give in to any tender feelings for a man whose only real interest in me is to get his hands on a canyon."

After taking a couple of aspirin, she dressed and went down to the kitchen.

"You look terrible," Helen said in a reproving tone. "As bad as Joe."

Maggie knew a confrontation was coming. She'd been expecting it. Helen lived in the house.

She had to feel the tension. With her mother-hen instincts toward Joe, she was bound to blame Maggie. Bracing for the onslaught of venom, Maggie said levelly, "Neither of us slept well last night."

The disapproval on Helen's face intensified. "I don't know what's going on. Maybe people are right. Maybe there's just something in the genes that won't let a Colbert and a Randolph live in peace together. But whatever is going on, you and Joe have got to work out a solution. You might be able to fool everyone else, but I can see through that act you put on for others. You're both miserable."

Surprised by Helen's fairness, Maggie let her guard slip. She'd been planning to deny any and all of the woman's accusations. Now she said, "We're trying to work it out."

"Well, you're going to have to work it out fast," the housekeeper said, worry replacing the disapproval in her voice. "Because it looks like Joe might be needing someone by his side to-day."

"Why?" Maggie demanded, her headache and exhaustion overshadowed by a surge of concern for Joe.

"He's out in the barn with the vet right now," Helen replied. "Lady Ann is having trouble giving birth. She's one of his favorite mares. He helped deliver her and now he might lose both her and her foal."

Before Helen had finished, Maggie was on her way out the back door. She was halfway to the barn when she heard the shot. Breaking into a run, she reached the building just as Joe came out. He was still holding the gun in his hand.

"Doc managed to save the foal," he said stiffly, in answer to the question in her eyes.

The pain on his face tore at Maggie's heart. "I'm sorry."

He nodded, then started toward the house.

Maggie had to jog to keep up with him, but she stayed by his side.

"Which one?" Helen asked anxiously as Joe entered the kitchen.

"Lady Ann," he answered without slowing his stride.

Take care of him, Helen's eyes ordered Maggie as she followed him.

"I need to be alone, Maggie," he growled as he reached his study door and realized she was still with him.

"No you don't." Ignoring the dismissal in his voice she entered the study with him.

Kicking the door closed, he crossed the room and dropped the gun on his desk. "Damn!" he cursed. Picking up the paperweight in front of him, he threw it into the fireplace. The sound of breaking glass filled the room.

Self-accusation showed on his features. "I bred her too soon."

Maggie moved to stand beside him. "No, you didn't," she said firmly.

He looked down at her cynically. "Are you suddenly an expert on horse breeding?"

"No," she answered, meeting his gaze evenly. "But I know you wouldn't have done anything on purpose to harm the mare."

A bitter smile tilted a corner of his mouth. "I almost believe you mean that."

She couldn't stand the suffering she saw in his eyes. Reaching up, she touched the hard line of his jaw. "I do mean it. You're a good man, Joe Colbert, and I'll stand against anyone who says differently."

"Maggie?" His voice was low and questioning as his gaze narrowed searchingly on her face.

She licked her suddenly dry lips. Maggie knew she should turn away before this went any further, but she couldn't. He needed someone to hold him and she wanted to be that someone. The surprise in his eyes, and then the warmth, told her he'd read her invitation and wanted to accept. *You're only asking for trouble,* her little voice warned and she knew it was right. But she couldn't fight the strength of her feelings for him. She had loved him all those years ago and she loved him now. It wasn't smart, but it wasn't something she had any control over.

"Maggie," he said her name again in a low, harsh whisper as his hands cupped her face and his mouth found hers.

It was a gentle kiss, and yet her whole body felt on fire. The blood rushed through her veins and the desire he had stirred before came alive again with an intensity that made her tremble.

"Sorry," he apologized gruffly, straightening away from her.

"There's no reason to apologize," she managed.

Again he searched her face and looked surprised by the messages he saw there. "Maybe not," he murmured. "I thought you trembled because you felt repulsed, but the look in your eyes could melt the ice cap at the North Pole.''

Flushing with embarrassment, Maggie dropped her eyes to the ground. She didn't want to be that obvious.

For a long moment he studied her in silence, then he said tersely, ''For six weeks you've treated me as if I had the plague. Now all of a sudden you do a complete turn around. You want to tell me what's going on?''

Determined to convince him that her sudden willingness was nothing more than a physical attraction, she said, ''You were right. I do still have physical needs. I've just been denying them.'' Afraid he might read how much she cared, she lowered her eyes again as she added, ''You need someone to hold you right now and I'd like to be that someone.''

His finger traced the line of her jaw. ''Are you sure, Maggie?'' he questioned as if he found this change in her almost impossible to believe.

A wave of fear suddenly swept over her. She ignored it. ''I'm sure,'' she replied.

He hesitated for a minute then said huskily, ''Maybe we should finish this discussion upstairs.''

"Maybe we should," she agreed, again ignoring her fear. It was time to put the past behind her! Joe needed her. *He needs a warm, soothing body to hold,* she corrected. Her jaw tightened. Well, she didn't care if it didn't matter to him who he held; she wanted to be the one who was with him.

Joe's eyes darkened with purpose. "I think definitely we should." Scooping Maggie up in his arms, he carried her out of the study and up to their bedroom. He stood her on the floor beside the bed, then closed and locked the door. "Wouldn't want any interruptions," he said coming back to stand in front of her.

"Nope," she replied, beginning to feel dizzy. Realizing she was hyperventilating, she took a couple of deep breaths.

Unhurriedly as if wanting to savor the moment, Joe began to unbutton her shirt. His fingers brushed against her, sending rivulets of fire racing across her skin. Nervously she watched his face as he slipped off her shirt and tossed it onto a chair.

When she saw her own longing mirrored in his eyes, she breathed a sigh of relief. He was not disappointed.

Unbuttoning his shirt, Maggie trailed kisses along the line of exposed flesh. He tasted sweet, and she delighted in the feel of the crisp hairs on his chest beneath her palms.

When his shirt had been discarded, he took over again. Her bra fell to the floor and as he drew her up against him and their lips met, the feel of flesh against flesh filled her senses until she thought her body was going to burst into flame.

His breathing grew ragged and, straightening away from her, he sat her on the bed and took off her boots. It tickled when he took off her socks and she giggled. Then he nipped her toes and fire spread up her legs. Next came her jeans and the fire blazed.

"You are beautiful," he said as he finished undressing her and she trembled with pleasure.

Lifting her in his arms, he laid her on the bed. Then after stripping off the rest of his clothing, he lay down beside her.

Maggie moved easily into his arms. But as she felt his need grow, old memories assaulted her. She tried to push them back but they refused to retreat. In spite of how much she wanted him, her body stiffened and a cold sweat broke out on her brow and the palms of her hands.

Joe's hand, which was moving caressingly along the curves of her body, stopped its sensual exploration.

She knew he felt her withdrawal. Furious with herself, she reached out to touch him reassuringly but a cold shiver shook her and her hands balled into defensive fists.

Levering himself up on an elbow, he looked searchingly into her face.

She tried to hide the fear and uncertainty she was feeling, but the effort was useless. Helplessly she watched his passion turn to controlled anger.

"What happened?" he demanded scornfully. "Did you think you could close your eyes and pretend I was Sam? Then at the last minute did you realize no mere mortal man could take his place?"

Maggie tried to speak but the words wouldn't come.

As if he found touching her suddenly distasteful, he released her. "I'm going to take a cold shower which is what I should have done in the first place," he growled. "I never did believe in three adults sharing a bed, even if one of them was a ghost."

As he strode into the bathroom and slammed the door behind him, Maggie rose from the bed and pulled on her robe. Now she had really done it! An icy chill shook her as the memories continued to fill her mind and a tiny trickle of tears rolled down each cheek. She had tried to put Sam behind her. He was dead and buried. She should be able to let go of the past. Hadn't she suffered enough?

Leaning against the wall and looking out the window, Maggie knew Joe had to be hating her. "He's probably cursing the day he let a Randolph step over his threshold."

A drop of wetness hit her hand and she realized the tears were still flowing down her cheeks. Angrily she brushed them away. She hadn't cried in years. Crying hadn't helped then and it wouldn't help now.

Staring out the window with unseeing eyes, she stopped fighting and let the memories invade her with full force.

"I thought you would be gone," Joe said, coming out of the bathroom. His tone implied that he had wanted her to be gone, that her being there was an invasion of his privacy.

"Sorry," she said, the word barely more than a whisper. She ordered her body to move. She would go in the guest room and wait until he left, then come back and dress. But her legs refused to work. She felt numb all over.

Pulling on a pair of jeans, Joe glared at her. "Figured you'd be out building some sort of monument to the wonderful Sam Hagan."

Maggie's jaw tightened and her eyes glazed over with visions she wanted to forget. "Sam Hagan was a horrible human being."

Joe paused with one arm halfway into the sleeve of his shirt. Frowning in disbelief, he stared at her. "What did you say?"

Until his question, Maggie hadn't even realized she had spoken aloud. She would have flushed but she felt too drained. Shrugging a shoulder as if to say what she had just said was unimportant, she continued to vacantly study the view beyond the window; remembered pain still filling her mind.

Joe shoved his arm the rest of the way into his sleeve as he crossed the room in long strides.

Coming to a halt in front of Maggie, he looked hard into her face. "Repeat what you just said."

She shifted her gaze to him, then back to the window. She'd never told anyone the truth. Maybe it was time. Maybe telling someone was the only way to rid herself of the nightmares that continued to haunt her. She tried to speak, but her vocal cords refused to respond.

"Either you tell me or I'm going to talk to your grandfather," Joe threatened.

"He doesn't know the truth, either," she heard herself saying.

"And what *is* the truth, Maggie?" Joe coaxed.

"My marriage to Sam Hagan was a living hell," she replied quietly, her eyes taking on a haunted quality as ugly visions continued to fill her mind.

"Talk to me, Maggie," he persisted gently.

She shuddered, then her face became grim. "I was in a rebellious mood when I met him. I knew my grandfather loved me, but he wanted me under his thumb and I was tired of his tyrannical rule." She didn't add that she had still been hurting from Joe's rejection of her in favor of his family. That was past history. Besides, her marriage wasn't his fault. She'd done it on her own and she had only herself to blame. "Sam was handsome and charming. He was a rodeo star with women constantly flirting with him. I was amazed and flattered when he showed an interest in me. When my grandfather objected to him, that only made me more determined to see him. Sam could be very romantic, and when he suggested we elope, I went with stars in my eyes. But those stars didn't last long." Maggie paused. Her mouth was dry and her palms damp. She wanted to stop but she couldn't. It was like lancing a wound. Now that it was opened, all the poison had to drain out.

"I realized very quickly that he had married me for the insurance money my parents left and the Double R Ranch he was certain I would inherit when my grandfather died." A sharp edge of bitterness entered her voice. "But I only had a small amount of the insurance money available to me. Most of it was in a trust I couldn't touch until I turned twenty-one or until my grandfather agreed to release it to me, whichever came first. And Gramps wasn't about to turn that money over to Sam Hagan. Sam was furious when he realized we weren't going to get the rest of the money for several years. He even went to my grandfather and tried to intimidate him into releasing it." A cynical smile played across her face. Sam was never a match for Frank. "That's when Gramps got mad and said he'd see that Sam never got the Double R Ranch, even if Gramps had to disown me. Sam was beside himself with anger." Maggie's stomach twisted into a knot and her hands balled into fists.

"What happened then, Maggie?" Joe asked when her pause threatened to lengthen into a silence.

She wanted to stop. What came next was deeply humilating. But she had come this far. There was no turning back now. "Sam took his anger and frustration out on me. He beat me pretty bad. I waited until the bruises on my face healed, then I left him. I was too proud to go back to my grandfather and admit what a fool I'd been, so I found a job as a waitress in a small café. But Sam found me and beat me again. Then he said if I ever tried to leave him again, he'd kill me." Hatred burned in Maggie's eyes. "There were times during those nine months we were man and wife when I thought death might be a welcome relief. I was planning another escape when that horse threw him and broke his neck. The tears I shed were ones of relief, not grief.''

Maggie fell silent and Joe studied her face. ''And you thought that if you gave in to me, I might start using you as a punching bag?'' he questioned grimly.

''No.'' Maggie shook her head to emphasize the word.

''Then why, Maggie? I know you weren't faking. You wanted me, then you drew away. If you didn't love Sam Hagan and you didn't think I would beat you, why did you suddenly act as if I was an ogre?''

Maggie felt nauseous.

''Tell me, Maggie,'' Joe coaxed. ''Get it all out or you'll be living with it forever.''

Maggie's chin trembled. She couldn't live with this any longer. Steeling herself, she said through clenched teeth, ''Sam was not a gentle man, especially when it came to being intimate. He taught me to associate intimacy with humiliation and pain.'' Scalding tears borne of years of pent-up fear, anger and humiliation refused to be held in check any longer. Escaping, they flowed down her cheeks in rivers.

"Everything's going to be all right, Maggie. You're safe here with me," Joe promised, stroking her hair. Lifting her into his arms, he carried her to the bed and laid her down gently.

Not wanting to see the pity in his eyes, she turned her face into her pillow and ordered herself to stop crying. But she couldn't. *You're behaving like a baby,* she scolded herself. But the tears refused to be controlled and the wrenching sobs continued.

She felt the bed move; Joe had laid down beside her.

"Seems like you could use a strong shoulder right about now," he offered.

Her pride demanded that she refuse his comfort. She didn't want his pity. But as he gently wrapped his arms around her, there was a warmth and security in his embrace she couldn't turn away from. Right now she needed it. Ignoring her pride, she curled up beside him and cried herself to sleep.

Hours later she awoke to the feel of a warm body against her cheek. Her eyes were sore and swollen from crying, and she knew she looked horrible. But even more embarrassing was the thought of everything she'd told Joe. She'd been too mortified and degraded by her experience with Sam Hagan to confess the truth to her grandfather and yet she'd told the whole ugly story to Joe.

"Are you feeling better?" a groggy male voice asked.

Combing the hair back from her face with her fingers, she said levelly, "Yes, thank you." Then, too embarrassed to face him, she slipped out of the bed and went into the bathroom without looking at him. She splashed cold water on her face, trying to get rid of some of the redness and swelling. It worked a little. Brushing her hair, she worked on building up her courage to face Joe. It was his pity she dreaded seeing the most.

A knock sounded on the door. "You all right in there?" he questioned from the other side.

"Fine," she called back. Frowning at her pale image in the mirror, she took a deep breath. She couldn't avoid him forever. Opening the door, she stepped back into the bedroom.

He was leaning against the wall waiting. Taking another deep breath, she met his gaze. But the pity she so dreaded seeing wasn't there. Instead she saw only deep concern. "You sure you're all right?" he asked.

"I'm sorry about unloading my nightmares on you," she apologized nervously, fighting a losing battle to control the scarlet flush of embarrassment that threatened to creep up her neck to her face.

"I didn't mind," he replied. "You needed to get it out of your system."

Sam had made her feel used and dirty. Now that Joe knew the truth, she wondered if he saw her that way, too. Afraid of what she might read in his face if she studied it too long, she turned away from him and walked over to the window. "Thanks for listening," she said, standing with her back toward him. "I promise you I won't bore you with any of my problems again."

"I wasn't bored," he assured her, adding tersely, "I'm just real sorry you had to go through an experience like that."

Pity! It had been there after all. A fresh wave of humiliation swept over her. She had to get out of here. "The day's almost gone," she said, "I'd better get dressed and go see Gramps. He'll be wondering what happened to me."

But as she started to gather her clothes, Joe placed a gently restraining hand around her arm.

"There is one little matter I want to clear up between us."

"What?" she asked, her guard immediately in place. She had opened herself up too much already today.

"I'm curious about what prompted your actions this morning. Now that I understand your fear, I'm finding it hard to understand why you were willing to try to let me make love to you."

He was studying her so intently she had to fight to keep from squirming under his gaze. She couldn't let him guess that her action had been prompted by love. "I told you. Living with a man had stirred up needs I thought I had managed to bury. According to the local gossips, you're very good at satisfying a woman. I was hoping your skills would work on me. I don't want to be afraid anymore. I want to be normal. I want to feel like a whole woman. And I thought if we had a physical relationship it would make the time we have together pass with less strain. I didn't move in here to make you feel uncomfortable." She was about to add that Helen would be happier if there was less tension, too, but stopped herself. If you give him any more reasons, they are going to start sounding like excuses, she cautioned.

For a long moment he studied her in silence, then said, "If you're still interested, I'm willing to try to work past your fear."

He still wanted her? She'd been certain he wouldn't want to go to the trouble of trying to pursue an intimacy between them once he knew how difficult it might be. "You're still interested?" she heard herself saying in disbelief.

"I'd like to prove I can live up to my reputation," he replied dryly.

She felt a sharp jab of pain. It was his ego that was prompting the offer. Well, she couldn't have expected a personal interest. From the beginning there had been nothing personal about this marriage, at least where Joe was concerned. Pride prodded her to refuse but she didn't want to turn back now. She had been honest when she said she wanted to put her fears behind her and feel like a whole woman again. And, her instincts told her that Joe might be the only man who could do that for her. "I am interested," she admitted. "But I'm not sure I can overcome those old nightmares. They've been with me a long time."

A smile tilted the corners of his mouth. "I'm a man who loves a challenge."

Looking up into his warm dark eyes, desire reawakened with a force that startled her. "I hope you win," she said.

"I intend to," he assured her. To give credence to his words, his mouth found hers for a long, slow kiss.

When he lifted his head, she saw the passion in his eyes. For a long moment she held her breath wondering what he would do next. A part of her wanted him to kiss her again while another part was hesitant and afraid it would end in disaster as it had earlier.

Reading the uncertainty in her eyes, he dropped a light kiss on the tip of her nose to tell her he understood. Then, stepping away from her, he said, "You'd better go see Frank before he comes looking for you."

Chapter Five

Later, while riding back to the Wild Stallion Ranch after her visit with her grandfather, Maggie wondered how Joe planned to meet the "challenge" she had provided him with.

He was down by the corral next to the barn when she rode in. Coming to a halt beside him, she saw the sadness on his face, then she saw the new foal in the corral. "She's beautiful," she said gently.

"Yeah," he agreed, continuing to watch the young filly prance around the enclosure. "She's almost a twin to her mother." Then looking up at Maggie, he said. "But it's never good to dwell on the dead. You have to look to the living."

The look in his eyes told her it was a message meant for both of them. She dismounted and as he walked with her to the barn, she saw the sorrow on his face lighten. She wanted to believe her company helped ease the pain of his loss, but she knew it was just the challenge she presented that was taking his mind off his grief. *And you'd better always remember that,* she warned herself. *You might love him, but he doesn't love you. I will,* she promised.

But it wasn't an easy promise to keep. She discovered Joe could be very romantic. During the next few days he brought her flowers and spent time with her. "I want you to learn to feel comfortable with me," he explained. "I know that's not an easy thing between a Colbert and a Randolph, but we can do it if we try."

Maggie forced a smile. Legally she might be Mrs. Colbert, but clearly Joe still considered her a Randolph. *You can't expect him to feel any different,* she chided herself. *This marriage is a business deal, not a love match.*

He also started sharing the bed with her again.

"I thought you should get used to having me here," he'd said that first night, then, kissing her gently, he'd rolled over and gone to sleep.

Maggie, on the other hand, had lain awake for nearly an hour. She ached to have him hold her, but she was terrified of making a fool of herself by suddenly drawing away from him again.

For two weeks Joe treated her purely as a friend. Maggie was beginning to think he'd lost interest in having a more intimate relationship with her. Then one morning he announced they were going on a picnic.

On the way to the spot he'd chosen, he spoke, as he had for the past weeks, about general subjects—the weather, work that needed to be done on the ranch, an interesting news item he'd seen on television. But Maggie noticed a subtle difference in him. *Maybe I'm just imagining it,* she mused, trying not to let her hopes build. Maybe it would be better if he *had* lost interest, she told herself for the hundredth time. This marriage wasn't going to last forever and she was afraid of the love she felt growing even stronger. She glanced at him and desire stirred within her. After all these years of nightmares, she deserved a few good memories to carry with her, she reasoned, and put the debate out of her mind.

They rode to a small mesa and climbed to the top.

"You do believe in giving a girl a workout before you feed her," she said, panting to catch her breath as they reached the flat summit.

"I've heard it said that physical activity helps relax a person," he replied, adding in a suggestive drawl, "Of course, I'd prefer a different kind of work out, but I don't want to appear impatient."

Her heart did a little flip-flop at the implication in his words. "So you brought me on a romantic mountain climbing expedition," she bantered back. A muscle suddenly spasmed in her leg and leaning over to rub it, she added, "I think I'm going to be more sore than relaxed when we get back home."

"Then I'll have to give you one of my famous massages," he returned in the same suggestive drawl. "I've been told I have the best hands in the west."

"I'll bet you have." She had to fight to keep the edge of jealousy out of her voice. For him this was to be strictly an impersonal affair with no strings attached, and jealousy didn't fit into that picture.

Setting aside the picnic basket, he approached her. "Just in case you have any doubts, let me ease your mind." Lifting her arms, he placed them around his neck. Then with an easy but firm movement, he began to massage her back, slowly moving along the curves of her body.

A sensual excitement spread through her. As his touch moved lower, her legs weakened and she tightened her hold on his neck molding her body to his. "You do have a very good sense of touch," she managed to say and wondered how the words had come out so coherently when she was having such a hard time thinking beyond the feel of him.

He smiled with satisfaction. "I'm glad I was able to prove that point to you." Dropping a light kiss on her lips, he unwound her arms from his neck and began spreading out the blanket for their picnic.

For a moment Maggie felt deserted. Then she scowled at herself. At least he was still interested. He was just moving slowly because he didn't want another disaster like the first time she'd offered herself to him. And she didn't want that either! However, she was getting anxious to get beyond this getting-to-know-you stage.

As the day progressed, it became clear that Joe had also decided it was time to take a more determined step. A part of her became alive with anticipation while another part began to worry. What if she couldn't respond? What if her fears won again?

Relax! she ordered herself. But just telling herself to do it didn't work.

It was late afternoon when they got back to the ranch and Joe had to check on some work down at the corrals. After promising her another of his expert massages later that night, he gave her a kiss that left no doubt he had more than a simple back rub in mind. Then he left.

Up in their bedroom, Maggie paced the floor. She didn't want another disaster, but she couldn't relax. Finally she decided she needed a little help to ease her anxiety; she drove into town and purchased two bottles of champagne. She'd only meant to buy one, but her palms had suddenly gotten sweaty and she'd grabbed a second. "Champagne in bed always works in the movies and on the soaps," she told herself encouragingly as she drove home.

"Looks like you're planning to do a bit of celebrating," Helen observed as Maggie put the bottles in the refrigerator.

"It's the anniversary of our first date," Maggie lied, knowing Helen would persist until she had some reason for the sparkling wine.

The housekeeper smiled, then shook her head. "I still can't get over the two of you seeing each other and nobody guessing. Or for that matter, just the two of you seeing each other." The housekeeper's smile broadened. "But it does seem to be working out well, after all."

Too nervous to enter into a conversation that could end up in a web of lies, Maggie merely smiled back and escaped. She was sitting in the living room trying to relax by reading a book when Joe entered the room.

"Do you have any idea what Helen is so worked up about?" he asked. "When I came in she met me at the door and said she hoped I hadn't forgotten. When I asked, 'forgotten what?' she just shook her head and went off muttering something about men having no romance in their souls."

Maggie blushed slightly. "I bought some champagne this afternoon. Lov—" She caught

herself halfway through the word. She and Joe
weren't lovers. He didn't love her. "In the soaps
and movies, people who are about to have an intimate encounter, a lot of times, seem to have
champagne or some kind of wine in bed. I
thought it might help—" she stopped herself just
as she was about to say "help me relax" and finished stiffly with "—create a romantic atmosphere."

A hint of impatience entered Joe's eyes. "I
don't think the champagne is going to help much
if you can't even say the word 'lovers' in reference to us."

"I rephrased it so you wouldn't begin to worry
that I might be expecting some kind of commit-
ment from you," she explained stiffly, suddenly
worried he would lose all patience with her and
decide she wasn't worth the challenge. "I don't
want you to think that I've forgotten that anything that happens between us is strictly non-
binding."

"I appreciate your concern." The impatience
disappeared as a self-mocking smile tilted one
corner of his mouth. "And you're right. We
certainly aren't traditional lovers. It's just a little hard on my male ego to think of myself as

merely an instrument of therapy to get you over a traumatic past experience.''

"I didn't mean it that way." Why did she always say the wrong thing where Joe was concerned? "I was only trying to assure you that I understand we are nothing more than two consenting adults who are planning to have some enjoyable sex with no strings attached," she explained tightly.

"An uninvolved affair," he said dryly.

"An uninvolved affair," she confirmed.

He was studying her in a way that made Maggie nervous. She saw an uncertainty in his eyes and her fear that he was losing interest grew stronger.

The uneasy silence between them was suddenly interrupted by a quick knock on the door, followed by Helen's entrance. "I've made plans to spend the night at my sister's," she announced. Sensing the heavy atmosphere in the room, she glanced at Joe and frowned. "You forgot, didn't you," she said accusingly. Shaking her head, she muttered something about men and romance under her breath and left the room.

Joe frowned at the closing door. "Would you please tell me what I have forgotten?" he demanded.

"She saw me putting the champagne in the refrigerator," Maggie answered, feeling the tension building even stronger between them. "She seemed to need some reason for it so I told her this was the anniversary of our first date."

"We have certainly woven a fabric of lies around ourselves," he muttered.

"I suppose so," she admitted, guessing he was thinking back to the day her grandfather had summoned him to his bedside. *If Joe had it all to do over again, I bet he wouldn't play along this time,* she mused tiredly.

When he turned back toward her, Joe's expression was unreadable. "About tonight," he said, "I think it's too soon. I think we should return to our neutral corners for a while."

He was rejecting her, and it hurt more than she had imagined anything could hurt. But pride refused to allow her to show any reaction. "I agree," she said evenly.

His gaze swung around the room, reminding her of a trapped animal. "I have a mare I need to check on," he said, and left.

Watching him go, Maggie knew the mare was only an excuse to escape her company. "And I'd better not hold my breath waiting for him to come out of his neutral corner again," she murmured tiredly. Maybe Helen was right. Maybe there was something in the genes that prevented Colberts and Randolphs from ever crossing that final line and getting close to one another.

Joe's presence was strong in the house. Needing to get away from it, she went for a ride, hoping that would ease the depression she was feeling. It didn't. She tried telling herself this was for the best and added sarcastically that Joe's lovemaking abilities were probably overrated. That didn't help, either. The moment the thought went through her mind, she remembered the touch of his hands and the pain of rejection came back twice as strong. "Damn!" She cursed herself for still wanting him.

Returning to the house, she stopped by the kitchen. To her relief, Helen wasn't there. On the counter was a note from the housekeeper wishing Joe and Maggie a happy anniversary and giving instructions on how to heat the casserole she'd left in the refrigerator.

"To happy anniversaries," Maggie muttered, opening the refrigerator and taking out a bottle of champagne. Joe wasn't interested in sharing it with her, but it would be a shame to let it go to waste. She found a crystal goblet. "Want to do this in style," she informed the empty kitchen. Carrying the bottle and the glass, she went upstairs to bathe. She'd never been one to drink much and certainly not alone, but this was a special occasion. She'd opened herself up and allowed Joe Colbert to reject her for a second time. Normally she never allowed herself to indulge in self-pity. She considered it a waste of time and energy. But at this moment she didn't care about the futility of it. Everything in her life had gone wrong and she didn't have the will nor the energy to pretend any different.

"This should teach me once and for all to stay away from men," she said with a self-directed scowl as she popped the cork on the champagne. "They're nothing but trouble." She added bubble-bath to the water filling the tub. Then she stripped and, after climbing into the tub, poured herself a glass of the cold champagne. Sipping the wine, she tried not to think and slowly the world lost its focus and her muscles began to relax. The water was becoming tepid and she was halfway through the bottle when a knock sounded on the bathroom door.

"Maggie, are you in there?" Joe demanded from the other side.

"I am," she replied, the words coming out slightly slurred. Frowning at herself, she tried saying it again more distinctly. "I am." Her pronunciation was clearer this time and she rewarded herself with an approving smile.

"I'm going to put the casserole in to heat. Dinner will be ready in about half an hour," he informed her.

Maggie lifted up her arm as if to check her watch. Squinting her eyes to focus them, she peered at the mass of bubbles on her wrist. Realizing she wasn't wearing her watch, she gave a small shrug as if to say it didn't really matter what time it was and let her arm drop back into the water. Bubbles splashed onto her face. Frowning in annoyance as she tried to dry her cheeks with her wet hand, she glared at the door. "You eat. I don't feel like having dinner tonight."

"Are you ill?"

She smirked at the concern in his voice. *He's probably afraid I'll get sick and my grandfather will blame him,* she mused, then frowned at herself. That wasn't fair. She knew Joe would care if she were sick. He just didn't want her. "No, I'm not ill," she called back, adding haughtily, "I'm sulking and I want to do it alone. So go away!"

For a moment there was silence, then Joe's voice sounded again from the bedroom. "I'm not leaving until I'm sure you're all right. Your speech sounds a little slurred."

"It's nothing for you to concern yourself with," she told him. "I'm just having a little champagne." Reaching over the side of the tub, she picked up the bottle and poured more of the now warm wine into her empty glass. Then taking a sip, she faced the door defiantly. "I didn't see any reason for it to go to waste. Now go away!"

Again there was a momentary silence. Then she heard the doorknob turning. She smiled to herself. She'd remembered to lock it. From the other side she heard a curse then boot steps leaving the bedroom.

"Good riddance," she said, drinking a toast to Joe's departure.

But a couple of minutes later she heard him returning and her smile faded as she heard him working on the lock. It only took a couple of minutes before he had the door open. Entering the room, he picked up the nearly empty champagne bottle and scowled at it. Then setting it aside, he stared down at her reprovingly. "It's time for you to dry off and dry out."

"I'll decide for myself when that time has come," she informed him haughtily, swishing bubbles around in an uncoordinated attempt to preserve her modesty.

The scowl on his face deepened. "You're in no condition to make any decisions. Now give me that glass and climb out of that tub!"

She considered arguing but the water was getting cold and Joe looked really angry. No sense in fighting over a cold bath, she decided. "You go away and I'll get out," she bargained.

His expression grew even grimmer. "I'm staying right here to make certain you don't hurt yourself. Now hand me that glass before you drop it and get cut."

She glared at him. "I do not require any assistance, thank you. Please leave."

"Give me the glass, Maggie," he demanded again. "And get out of that tub."

Her gaze traveled up the long length of his body to the stubborn set of his jaw. *Now I know what an immovable mountain of a man looks like,* she thought acidly. Grudgingly she handed him the glass, but when she started to sit up, her head began to swim. Then she realized her legs felt numb. She wiggled her toes to assure herself that her feet were still attached. Unwilling to admit she was having coordination trouble, her mouth formed a petulant pout. "I'll get out of this tub when I'm ready, and I'm not ready now."

Cynical amusement replaced the reproval in Joe's eyes. "You can't get up, can you?"

"Of course I can," she hissed self-righteously. "And if you were a gentleman you'd leave a lady alone in her bath."

"This is really stupid." The impatient anger she had grown so used to seeing was again etched into his features. "You could fall and hit your head or break a bone. You could even drown."

The room was beginning to spin. Closing her eyes in an effort to maintain a semblance of control, she said tightly, "I am perfectly capable of taking care of myself."

"That remains to be seen." Setting the glass aside, he stood with his hands on his hips, frowning down at her. "You're going to have to prove that to me by getting out of that tub right now. And, if you don't get out on your own, I'm going to lift you out."

The thought of him lifting her out sent a warm current through her body. Furious with herself for her continued weakness for him, her jaw tightened. "All right," she snapped. "I'll get out." Deciding she had a better chance if there was no water, she lifted her leg and used her toe to release the drain. It took four tries before she was actually successful. "It's slippery and I don't function at my best when people are glaring at me," she said in her defense.

Joe made no comment. He simply stood in a stoic silence and watched the water drain out.

"You could at least throw me a towel," she said, acutely aware of her nakedness as the bubbles receded.

Taking a towel from the rack, he handed it to her.

Without looking at him, Maggie forced herself into a sitting position and wrapped the towel around her upper torso. But when she tried to rise further, her legs felt like rubber. Putting her hands on the side of the tub, she tried to use them as levers but her arms felt like rubber, too.

Continuing to regard her darkly, Joe pulled the shower curtain into place and turned on the cold water.

"Stop that!" she sputtered, her body shivering as the icy water cascaded over her. But Joe made no move to help her. It only took a couple of minutes but it seemed like forever before she could move well enough to turn off the water herself.

As soon as the shower stopped, Joe pulled back the curtain. Placing his hands around her waist, he lifted her to her feet. The soaked towel remained in the bottom of the tub and she saw his frown darken further at her nakedness. Grabbing another towel from the rack, he wrapped it around her and then lifted her out of the tub.

Pride kept her chin up in spite of the headache building at her temples. "Put me down," she demanded as he carried her into the bedroom.

"Gladly," he said, coming to a halt by the bed and dropping her onto it.

Groaning, Maggie closed her eyes and fought back a wave of nausea caused by the motion of the bed. Then as the world began to settle around her, she opened her eyes slowly. Joe was staring down at her with that disapproving look still on his face. Shifting her gaze away from him, she focused her eyes on her toes. "My feet are pickled," she muttered unhappily, trying not to think about Joe standing over her.

"So is your stomach," he added pointedly.

"Just go away!" she ordered again. "You don't want to be here and I don't want you here!" In a terrible Greta Garbo impersonation she added, "I vant to be alone."

Ignoring her command, Joe continued to regard her grimly. "I can't believe you actually sat in that tub and drank yourself into this condition."

Another wave of nausea washed over her and her head began to throb. "And I can't believe how bad I feel," she said with a low moan. "I thought alcohol was supposed to relax a person and ease the pain."

"You're way past relaxed," he informed her dryly. "You're limp."

"And really tired," she added, crawling under the covers and falling promptly to sleep.

The room was dark when she woke. The clock on the bedside table told her it was nearly 3:00 a.m. Her head ached and when she lifted it off the pillow it felt like a two-ton weight. Feeling as if she were facing a major challenge, she ordered herself to get out of bed. Making her legs move, she kicked the sheet off, then grabbed it back up when she realized she had nothing on. Embarrassment brought a flush to her cheeks as she recalled her antics of the past evening. She seemed to have developed a real knack for making a fool of herself. Hearing a light snore, she glanced over her shoulder and saw Joe asleep on the far side of the bed. That he was there at all surprised her. *Of course, he's as far from me as he can get,* she noted sarcastically.

Pushing Joe out of her mind, she raked a hand through the tangled mass of her hair, combing it out of her face. Then, very carefully, she climbed out of the bed and made her way to the bureau. There she opened a drawer and found a nightgown. Pulling it on, she had to stifle a groan. Every movement caused her head to throb.

In the bathroom, she found the aspirin but no water glass. "I wanted orange juice anyway," she muttered.

Down in the kitchen she found a glass. She was opening the refrigerator to get out the orange juice when Joe came in.

"Feeling any better?" he asked, disapproval still strong in his voice.

She caught a quick look at herself in the mirror by the door and groaned mentally. Her hair was a mess and her complexion ashen. "I feel better than I look," she answered honestly.

Joe frowned at the open refrigerator. "I hope you aren't down here to get that second bottle of champagne."

"No, I'm going to use some orange juice to take a couple of aspirin," she replied tersely, furious that he would think she would be so stupid as to repeat her earlier performance. Becoming mobile again, she took the juice out of the refrigerator.

He continued to watch her narrowly. "It's clear you can't handle liquor. You could've hurt yourself. What in the hell did you think you were doing?"

Avoiding looking at him, she poured the orange juice into a glass, then used it to swallow the two aspirin while she tried to remember what she'd said to him earlier in the evening. But the events were foggy. Forcing a nonchalance into her voice, she said, "Everyone has their bad moments."

"Do you go on these drinking binges often?" he asked contemptuously.

Pride glistened in her eyes. Turning toward him she said icily, "I've never gone on one before and I don't intend to ever go on one again." To her relief her jaw muscles seemed to be functioning more normally and her head didn't feel so heavy.

"I'll take your word on that," he conceded. Still the disapproval remained on his face. "But I still can't understand why in the world you would do something so stupid."

"Because I had a bad reaction to rejection," she said, seething, then flushed when she realized what she'd said. Drawing a shaky breath, she schooled her face into what she hoped was a look of cool detachment. "But now that I've had time to think about it, you're absolutely right. The idea of an intimacy between us—a Colbert and a Randolph—is absurd. Neutral corners is where we belong."

For a long moment a heavy silence hung between them. Then self-consciousness replaced the disapproval in his eyes as he said gruffly, "That's not what I want. It was my ego talking this afternoon. First you made it sound as if any male with the right equipment would suit your purposes. Then there was your purchase of the wine. No man likes to think a woman has to get drunk to be able to let him touch her."

"When I bought the champagne I didn't plan to get drunk on it," she defended tightly. "I admit I was a little nervous but that was only natural under the circumstances. I just thought a small amount would relax me. And I *never* said that just any man would do." She regarded him with dignity. "I am not the promiscuous type."

"I know you're not." Joe's features softened. Approaching her, he began to gently massage her neck.

Pride insisted that she move away from him, but the feel of his hands was sending soothing currents through her head and shoulders and she had no will to resist his healing touch.

"Come back up to bed and sleep some more," he coaxed. "In the morning, when you feel better, I'll try to convince you to forgive me."

There was a promise in his voice that started her heart beating more rapidly. Don't do it, her little voice warned. Think of how hurt you're going to be when he walks away from this marriage with the deed for White Horse Canyon and barely a glance in your direction. But she didn't listen. She'd allowed the fear of the past to make her life miserable. She would not let the fear of the future stop her from finding some pleasure in the present.

When she offered no resistance, he picked her up, carried her back upstairs and tucked her back into bed. Climbing in beside her, he held her in the protective circle of his arms. "Sleep," he ordered.

Lying snuggled up against him, she obeyed.

The sun was up when she awoke again. She felt Joe beside her and remembered her antics of the evening before—and her confession of feeling rejected. Embarrassment began to build in her. But when she opened her eyes all thought was lost.

He was propped up on an elbow, watching her and the soft, dark depths of his eyes told her he planned to keep the promise of the night before. "How do you feel?" he asked, very slowly combing the stray hairs from her face.

The residue of her headache vanished as his touch sent tiny rivulets of fire racing across her skin. "Better."

"I've heard it said that a little stimulation, something that gets the adrenaline pumping, is a great cure for a left over hangover," he said, dropping light kisses on her face.

"I never heard that," she replied, her blood racing hotly as his hand moved across her abdomen, then upward to explore the firm roundness of her breast. "But I suppose it's worth a try."

"It's definitely worth a try," he assured her as his mouth found hers.

He didn't rush. He kissed and caressed her until her body ached for his. But as much as she wanted him, she felt herself withdrawing when he began to possess her. He sensed it, too, and she felt his muscles tighten as he restrained himself.

"Please, don't stop," she urged, fighting her fear.

His gaze narrowed on her in concern. "Are you sure?"

She heard the strain of his control in his voice. If she was going to turn back this would be her last chance. But she didn't want to turn back. She wanted to put the past behind her. "I'm sure," she said.

Later as she lay beside him, she felt as if a whole new world had opened up to her. He'd brought her body to a level of excitement and pleasure she'd never believed possible.

"Penny for your thoughts," he said, levering himself up on an elbow so he could look down into her face.

She saw the worry in his eyes and smiled reassuringly. "I was just thinking that you more than lived up to your reputation."

Relief replaced the worry and he smiled back. "And how about your hangover?"

"Gone," she answered, then added hesitantly, "But I wouldn't mind a second treatment just to make certain I don't have a relapse."

The smile on his face broadened and the brown of his eyes darkened. "I'll be more than happy to accommodate you," he assured her.

Fire spread through her veins. *Just keep remembering this is only a physical relationship,* her little voice cautioned. *I will,* she promised with her last rational thought as he began to carry her away into a world of delicious sensation once again.

Chapter Six

But it wasn't an easy promise to keep. In spite of all her efforts to the contrary, her feelings for Joe grew stronger with each passing day and she was tormented by thoughts of the loneliness she would feel when they parted. She would be all alone then. Not only would she not have Joe any longer, but her grandfather would be gone, too.

"I could always remarry," she muttered under her breath one sunny day as she watched Lady Anne's foal frolicking around in the corral. But this thought left her cold. Joe was the only man she wanted. She'd tried to deny that once and ended up with Sam Hagan. She wouldn't make that mistake again.

Watching the young horse, she admitted to herself that what she really wanted was a child— Joe's child. It would be a part of him she could take with her, a part she could love openly with no reservations. And it would give her the family she wanted and not leave her alone or forced by loneliness into a marriage that wouldn't touch her heart. The problem was, she didn't know how Joe would react. He was a man with a strong sense of family. He might be able to walk away from her, but he couldn't turn away from his child and she didn't want him to feel trapped, bound to a woman he didn't love for the sake of a child.

"We could work it out," she said aloud as if saying it would make it so. The little colt stopped prancing and looked at her. "We can," she said more firmly.

All day she debated about how to approach Joe. At first she considered the possibility of simply getting pregnant and dealing with Joe's anger afterward. But that was the cowardly thing to do, and besides, she loved him too much to put him in that situation.

"You about ready to tell me what's bothering you?" he asked as they sat across from one another at the dinner table that night.

"Nothing's bothering me," she lied.

"You've rearranged every piece of food on your plate but you haven't taken a bite," he pointed out. "Since it can't be Helen's cooking that's put your appetite off, either you're sick or you're worried about something. Which is it?"

She looked up at him and in her mind she saw herself holding a little boy with those same brown eyes. Talk to him, she ordered herself. She licked her suddenly dry lips. "There is something on my mind."

His gaze traveled from her to her full plate of food then back to her. "Looks to me as if you need to talk to someone about it."

"I need to talk to you," she said firmly, the words more of an order to herself than a response to him.

"Go on," he coaxed when she fell silent.

Maggie's eyes wandered to the kitchen door. She didn't want Helen to come in suddenly and hear their conversation. This was much too private and could be embarrassing if Joe didn't want her to have his child. "Could we go into your study?" she asked.

Following her line of vision, he frowned. "I take it this is serious." His expression became unreadable. Rising from the table, he motioned for her to precede him out of the room.

Once they reached his study, she waited until he closed and locked the door. Then she tried to speak, but all the words she had practiced suddenly jumbled together in her mind and she couldn't seem to form a coherent sentence.

"Well, what is on your mind?" he asked when her silence threatened to continue forever.

"This is a little hard," she said, marveling at how much of an understatement that was.

The frown returned to Joe's face as if he had already guessed he wasn't going to like what she had to say. "I suggest you simply take a deep breath and tell me."

She faced him evenly. She had to explain this just right. She couldn't let him guess how she felt about him. "When this marriage is over, I'll be all alone in the world. I don't exactly find that a happy prospect. So I've been thinking that I would like to have a child."

Shock registered on his face. "A child?" As if he had just realized the full implication of her words, he said gruffly, "*My* child?"

"*Our* child," she corrected. Before he could begin to worry about entanglements, she continued hurriedly, "But I wouldn't want you to feel any obligation to me or even the child if you're not really interested in fatherhood."

His face looked like the sky before a storm. "I would never turn away from my own child."

The last thing she wanted was to make him angry. "I didn't mean to say I thought you would," she explained quickly, adding with a touch of helplessness, "I just didn't know. I want the child but I want to be fair to you, too. I don't want you to feel you're being trapped."

His expression once again became unreadable. "And what are your plans for our child after the divorce?"

She wondered if he was really considering the possibility of their having a child or if he was merely being sarcastic. "We could have mutual custody, and since we would be neighbors you would be free to see him or her every day," she answered.

"So what you want is a sort of uninvolved pregnancy like our uninvolved affair," he said dryly.

Humiliation swept over her. He was making fun of her. He didn't want her to have his child. Her back stiffened with pride. "Forget it. It was a stupid idea," she said with controlled dignity. She moved toward the door in brisk, quick strides. Why was she always placing herself in a position of ridicule in front of him? Hot tears of self-directed anger burned at the back of her eyes. She had to get out of there before she made a bigger fool of herself.

Joe reached Maggie before she could unlock the door. His hands closed around her arms, and he turned her to face him. "I don't want to forget about it," he said tersely. "I would like to have an heir. Since this marriage of ours appears to be going to continue for a while, our having a child would be a reasonable way to get one."

He was agreeing! It wasn't the most flattering acceptance of fatherhood, but then she hadn't expected him to be overwhelmed with emotion at the thought of them having a child. In spite of their intimacy and the more relaxed manner in their attitude toward one another, a barrier still existed between them. There were moments when it almost became invisible, but Maggie never tried to fool herself into believing it would go away. To Joe she would always be a Randolph. For a brief moment, it occurred to her that she could be asking for real trouble if she continued with this but she wanted his child more than she had ever wanted anything. "A very reasonable way," she heard herself agreeing.

The brown of his eyes darkened. "I think we should get started on this right away."

The fire he so easily ignited within her burst into flames. "You haven't finished dinner," she reminded him, not wanting him to guess how much she wanted him.

"I finished my main course. You'll do for dessert," he replied, unlocking the door.

"I prefer to think of myself as a main course," she bantered back, wishing she could muster a bit more resistance toward him.

"You're a *full* meal," he assured her, slipping an arm around her waist and guiding her out of the study and up the stairs.

About four weeks later, Maggie began to find that the thought of food caused a wave of nausea, especially in the morning. That, together with her exhaustion, and the fact that she was two weeks late made her fairly certain she was pregnant. But she didn't want to say anything to Joe until she was absolutely certain. She made an appointment to see her doctor. He confirmed her pregnancy.

Driving home from his office, Maggie felt exhilarated. She was going to have a baby—Joe's baby. But when she thought of Joe, she grew a little apprehensive. He'd been somewhat distant for the past couple of days and she worried that he might have changed his mind about fatherhood. For a while she contemplated not telling him right away, but decided that would be stupid. He was bound to notice her body beginning to change and then he'd wonder why she hadn't told him right away. Besides, it didn't matter if he'd changed his mind; she hadn't. She wanted this baby.

She found him in his study when she got home. She tried to think of a clever way to tell him, but her ideas seemed appropriate only for couples in love. Finally, she settled for a simple statement of fact. ''I thought you might like to know I'm pregnant," she said, bracing herself in case his reaction was less than enthusiastic.

"I know." Remaining seated behind his desk, he studied her narrowly. "Or at least, I've been pretty certain for the past few days—ever since you turned green at the breakfast table the other morning." A flicker of anger escaped from behind his shuttered mask. "In fact, I've been wondering when you were going to tell me."

She stiffened defensively at the implied accusation that she had been purposely keeping it a secret. "I wanted to see the doctor first and have it confirmed before I said anything."

Rising from the desk, he approached her. "I would have taken you to see the doctor."

The controlled anger in his voice confused her. "I didn't see any reason for you to be inconvenienced."

"It would *not* have been an inconvenience." Coming to a halt in front of her, he looked hard into her face. "This child is mine as well as yours, Maggie, and I intend to be a very large part of its life. Don't you ever forget that or try to stop me."

That he still wanted the child was a relief, but that he did not trust her to be fair in sharing the parenting cut deeply. She should have expected this, she reasoned, trying to soothe the pain. There had never been any trust between the Colberts and the Randolphs. Meeting his gaze with level honesty, she said, "I wouldn't."

His anger faded to be replaced by concerned interest. "What did the doctor say? Does he expect any complications?"

"He says I'm fine healthy breeding stock," she assured him.

Joe smiled with relief. "Glad to hear that."

Maggie wanted him to take her in his arms and whirl her around. *But that's what people in love do, and we're not in love,* she reminded herself. Suddenly needing to be alone, she said, "I think I'll go upstairs and rest before dinner."

"One other thing." Joe moved into her path before she could make good her escape. "From now on I'll take you to see the doctor. I don't want you making that hour's drive alone."

Maggie considered telling him she wasn't an invalid. But the hard set of his jaw told her it would be useless. "It really isn't necessary," she said. "But if you want to come along, you're welcome."

"I do want to come," he replied, then moved out of her way.

Lying on the bed, she stared at the ceiling. At least Joe still wanted the child, she told herself, but she couldn't help wishing he wanted her, too. *You are only asking for trouble to dwell on what can never be,* she warned herself. She knew she should take this warning to heart, but it wasn't easy. The image of her, Joe and the baby as a loving, happy family tormented her.

"We'll turn the guest room next to our bedroom into a nursery," Joe announced at breakfast the next morning. "Then when the child's older, he or she can move into my old room. It's larger. Colbert children need plenty of elbow room." Maggie felt a rush of panic. The way Joe said "Colbert children" sounded very possessive. Was he thinking about fighting her for custody of the child? Then she began to breath again as he added, "I want our child to have a place in this house that he can consider his to return to whenever he wants to come visit overnight."

But while she was relieved, she had heard the defensive edge in his voice and realized that he thought she would fight him on this. How could he think she would be so cruel as to try to keep his child from him? But the fairness in her overpowered the anger. The answer was easy—because she was a Randolph. She remembered the blue ribbon she'd seen on the lamp in the bedroom her first day here. "I keep it to remind me that Colberts and Randolphs can never be anything at heart but enemies," he'd said. He'd removed the ribbon before the wedding but, clearly, he had kept the philosophy it represented. "You're right," she agreed, her voice free from reservation. "He should have a place that is his in his father's house."

Joe looked relieved and a little surprised. "You're being very fair and reasonable. I appreciate that."

"I told you I would be," she reminded him tersely, her patience with his lack of trust wearing thin. "If it would make you feel better we can shake on it."

"No, I'll take your word on it," he replied, adding gruffly, "I'm sorry. I just don't want you to forget this is my child, too."

"I've already promised you I won't." Now it was her turn to frown at him impatiently. "If it will keep a strain from developing between us, I'll sign an oath in blood."

He raked a hand through his hair. "I don't want you to feel under any strain. It's not good for you or the baby." He held a hand out toward her. "Truce?"

"Truce," she agreed, wondering how long it would last.

After breakfast, she went upstairs to see what would need to be done to the guest room. The bed would have to go and the lamps weren't right for a nursery. They were hurricane lamps and too easily breakable. The bureau and one of the small tables could stay.

Going down to the kitchen, she asked Helen if there was a convenient place to store the furniture they wouldn't be needing.

"There might be room in the attic," Helen said hopefully.

Maggie went to check. "It's going to require a little rearranging," she muttered, picking up a couple of boxes and shifting them farther into a corner. "And this table can go over there." It was a small round table with a lone cigar box sitting on top of it. Carrying the table and its contents to the far end of the attic, she was too concerned about tripping and falling to pay attention to the cigar box as it moved around slightly on top of the table. She accidentally tilted the table a little too far so she could see her footing better and the box fell to the floor. "Darn!" she cried. "I knew I should have taken that box off. I'm trying to clean up one mess and I've just created anoth..." Her words died abruptly as she knelt to pick up the spilt contents of the box.

The faded blue ribbon was there with a handful of blurred photographs—some of her and some of her and Joe together. They looked so young. "We *were*," she said softly, as bittersweet memories of those few short weeks of their teenage romance assailed her. She remembered the day the pictures were taken as if it were yesterday. Joe had gotten an expensive camera for his birthday and he'd brought it with him when they met for their ride. She remembered how shy she'd felt when he insisted on taking her picture and how much they laughed when he set the timer then tried to get into the picture with her before the shutter clicked. They'd had their fight before the pictures were developed and she'd never seen them. *Looks like they turned out about as well as our short-lived romance,* she mused with regret. Shaking off a sudden depression, she scooped up the rest of the photos and put them back in the box, along with the ribbon.

Scanning the dust-covered floor for anything else that might have fallen out, she spotted a flash of blue-green. Picking up the polished piece of turquoise, she chewed on her bottom lip as she rubbed off the dust. She had given it to Joe for his birthday. Her grandfather had given it to her. He'd told her he got it from an old Indian. It was supposed to bring luck to the person who possessed it. When she'd found out it was Joe's birthday, she wanted to give him something special, so she gave him the stone. Polishing it with the hem of her shirt, she glanced at the cigar box and wondered why Joe had kept these things. A ray of hope glimmered within her. Maybe, deep in his heart, he still cared.

"You can have it back. It's just collecting dust up here."

Startled, Maggie looked over her shoulder and saw Joe. She'd been so engrossed in old memories, she hadn't heard him approaching.

"You can have the stone back," he repeated.

Looking up at him, she tried to see past his mask of indifference but couldn't. That's probably because it isn't a mask, her little voice pointed out curtly. "No, thanks," she said, matching his show of indifference. "I don't believe in taking back a gift once it's given."

A cynical smile tilted at one corner of his mouth. "Afraid its luck's been ruined because it belonged to a Colbert?"

"No." Tossing the rock into the cigar box, she rose and dusted off her knees. "I just don't believe in luck anymore." Then embarrassed to have been caught going through a box of his private possessions, she said stiffly, "And I wasn't prying. I accidentally dropped the box while I was moving that table." She nodded toward the round table as proof of her story.

"I didn't accuse you of prying." Bending over, he picked up the box and frowned at the photos. "I should have thrown these out years ago. They're probably the worst pictures I ever took."

He said it as though they could have been pictures of cactus for all he cared. The ray of hope Maggie had been trying to keep alive died a swift death.

Setting the box aside, he frowned at her. "Helen told me you were already getting busy on the nursery. I don't want you doing any lifting or carrying. I'll get a couple of my men in here and you can tell us what you want moved."

Maggie matched his frown with one of her own. "Being pregnant doesn't make me an invalid."

"I just don't want to take any chances," he said in a reasoning tone. "Humor me, Maggie."

"You're being ridic—"

"I thought we had a truce," he interjected.

She really didn't want to fight with him. "All right. Get your men."

He rewarded her with a satisfied smile. "And while I'm getting them, why don't you go down to the kitchen and have a nice glass of milk? That way I won't worry about you doing any more rearranging up here while I'm gone." Stepping aside, he made a sweeping gesture with his arm to indicate he wanted her to leave the attic ahead of him.

Tossing him a disgruntled glance, she obeyed.

"He really is being ridiculous," she complained to Helen a few minutes later as she leaned against the counter watching the housekeeper knead bread. Joe had left her in Helen's charge while he went to find a couple of hands to help with the furniture.

"He's just concerned about your health," Helen replied. "Prospective fathers have been known to act a little overly protective. It's only natural."

Maggie had to admit she really wouldn't mind all the nursemaiding if she thought it was for her. But she knew Joe's real concern lay with the baby. *You're being petty,* her little voice chided. *You knew from the beginning the baby would be the most important thing to him. You can't suddenly decide to fault him now.* Admitting her little voice was right, she finished her milk with no further complaints.

As if he didn't trust her, Joe returned fairly quickly with the men and stayed to help with the moving.

When all the furniture they would not be needing was finally stored in the attic, Maggie turned her attention to what remained. "Everything else will have to go into the other guest bedroom for a while," she said. Joe shot her a questioning glance, and she added, "This room will have to have a thorough cleaning and I think it needs a new paint job."

He nodded in agreement and began moving the rest of the furnishings out of the room.

When the room was finally cleared, she went down to the kitchen for a bucket, scrub brush and sponge. As she backed out of the closet holding the cleaning supplies and turned around, she again found herself facing Joe.

"And what do you think you're doing now?" he questioned.

"I'm going to start cleaning the room," she replied matter-of-factly.

"No, you're not." His chin was set in a determined line. "I'll hire someone to do the cleaning and painting."

Maggie had promised herself she would not argue with him, but she was beginning to feel suffocated. "You really are being ridiculous," she said with tight control. "I cannot simply sit around and vegetate until this baby is born."

"You're going to take it easy and not do anything strenuous," he ordered.

The look in his eyes told her arguing would be useless. Relinquishing the cleaning supplies, she went into the kitchen and offered to help Helen fix lunch.

As she ate, she admitted to herself that she was procrastinating. She could have started getting the nursery ready anytime during the next five months. What she absolutely had to do today was to tell her grandfather about her pregnancy. She knew he wanted a great-grandchild, but she wasn't so certain how he would feel about one with Colbert blood running through its veins. Her mouth formed a hard, straight line. Well, it's what he's going to get and he better like it!

"News travels fast," Joe said, breaking into her thoughts. As if he had read her mind, he continued, "If you don't want Frank to find out about this pregnancy from someone else, we'd better go over and tell him this afternoon."

The "we" sent a wave of panic through her. "You're right. Gramps does need to be told this afternoon," she replied, trying to think of a diplomatic way to tell Joe she thought she should go alone to tell her grandfather.

Again as if reading her thoughts, he said firmly, "And I think both of us should be there. Whether he likes it or not, this child is half Colbert."

Maggie considered trying to convince Joe that it would be better if she went alone, but the hard set of his jaw told her it would be useless and only cause hard feelings. "Fine," she said evenly, praying silently that everything would go well.

Knowing her anxiety was only going to build, she decided it would be best to get this over with as quickly as possible. Right after lunch, she called the Double R to make certain her grandfather would be home, then she and Joe drove over to see him.

Frank frowned in surprise when Joe walked in with Maggie. "You two wouldn't be bringing me some good news, like maybe you've decided to call this marriage off," he asked pointedly.

Maggie scowled impatiently at her grandfather. "After a remark like that, I'm not sure you deserve to hear the news."

Frank's gaze narrowed on her. "You look different, gal. There's something about your eyes." Then a broad smile split his face. "You're going to give me a great-grandchild."

"*We're* going to have a child," Maggie said firmly, slipping her arm through Joe's to emphasize her point. Her grandfather had to understand that Joe was part of the child, too.

But Frank ignored Joe. "A new Randolph," he said with a pleased laugh.

"A Colbert," Joe corrected.

"A Randolph-Colbert," Maggie interjected quickly, flashing a warning glare at her grandfather.

"I suppose it does take two," Frank conceded grudgingly. Giving Maggie a hug, he added in a whisper for her ears only, "It doesn't matter who the father is, we both know the Randolph blood will win out."

Making a mental note to have a talk with her grandfather later, Maggie made no reply. She didn't want a fight in front of Joe, but she wasn't going to let her child get caught in the middle of this feud and end up hurt like she had been.

Releasing Maggie, Frank turned his attention to Joe. Instead of offering the traditional handshake, he said threateningly, "You'd better take good care of my granddaughter and my new great-grandchild or you'll have me to answer to."

"I'll take excellent care of *my* wife and *my* child," Joe replied tersely.

"Stop it, both of you," Maggie demanded in exasperation. Searching for some way to make both men behave, she said, "I'm not supposed to be under any strain. It's bad for the pregnancy. I want the two of you to promise me you'll stop this bickering and call a truce."

"I'm willing," Joe said, still regarding Frank grimly.

"It won't be easy, Maggie, but I'll try," Frank promised.

Maggie looked from one man to the other and wondered if there could ever be a real truce between them. There has to be, she decided firmly. For her child's sake she'd make certain there was.

The next morning Maggie rode over to the Double R to talk with her grandfather about Joe and the baby. But Frank was determined to be his usual unreasonable self where the Colberts were concerned.

"I'm happy you're having a child, gal," he said, "and I'll love it as if it has pure Randolph blood running in its veins. But to tell the truth, I wish I'd refused to let you marry a Colbert. It just doesn't sit right."

"It sits just fine," she said firmly. "You're just too bullheaded to admit that Joe is a good man."

Frank shook his head. "He's a Colbert and you can never be certain about a Colbert. They do what's best for them and to hell with everyone else."

"That's exactly what Joe thinks of the Randolphs," she snapped. Frank's gaze narrowed on her. She'd let her frustration cause her to make a serious slip. "That's what he thinks of you," she corrected quickly. It would never do for Frank to guess that Joe didn't trust her, either. Then there would never be any chance for peace between the two families. "For my sake, I want you to promise me you will be more tolerant of my husband."

"I already said I would," Frank reminded her.

"I know," she conceded. "But you don't seem to be trying very hard."

"Doing what ain't natural ain't easy," he replied.

"Promise me you'll try," she insisted.

"I'll try," he assured her. "But I ain't promising it'll work."

Over the next few days, Maggie had to admit that both men did try, but their distrust of one another was too deeply ingrained. On the surface they were polite, but when they were in the same room, the tension could be cut with a knife.

"What I don't understand is why two men who can be reasonable and rational with nearly everyone else in the world can't get along with one another," Maggie complained to Sarah on one of her visits to her grandfather. Frank had

just put her through a half-hour interrogation to
assure himself that Joe was treating her well.
Now she was sitting in the kitchen trying to calm
her nerves before going home.

"There are too many years of feuding and too
much family pride between them," Sarah said.
"You can't expect it to vanish overnight. The fact
that they can be in the same room and not end up
in a shouting match every time is a great im-
provement."

Maggie had to agree. For her child's sake, she
hoped Joe and her grandfather would become
even more tolerant of one another soon.

Back at the White Stallion Ranch, she found
Joe in his study using saddle soap on a child-size
saddle.

"It was my first saddle," he said, seeing her at
the door. "Been saving it for my child."

She sat down in one of the leather wing chairs
by the fireplace and watched him as he continued to work. He'd said he wanted the child simply because he wanted an heir, but what she was
watching was a labor of love. Sitting in the late
afternoon heat, she lazily pictured a couple of
children running around the room. Joe fit into
that picture very comfortably. "In spite of your

past resistance to marriage, you really are a family man at heart," she said, then flushed when she realized she'd spoken aloud.

There was a hint of amusement in his eyes as he glanced at her. "You think so? You can picture me with a nice little wife and a herd of kids?"

"As a matter of fact, I can," she answered honestly, feeling a sharp pain as she wished she could be that nice little wife, and the mother of that herd of kids.

"You could be right," he conceded in an easy drawl, returning his attention to the saddle.

"I am," she said without reservation. This brought up another question that had been on her mind a lot lately. Normally she would never have asked. She'd made it a practice to respect his privacy and not ask personal questions. But he was the father of her child and she decided it was time she understood him better. "And it makes me wonder why you never married before."

For a moment she sensed his hesitation, then he said with a shrug of indifference, "Maybe I never met a woman who was willing to put up with me."

Maggie frowned at him in disbelief. "I find that really hard to believe. I know half a dozen women who would have married you at the drop of a hat."

"I think you're exaggerating," he said with an amused smile.

She met his smile with a reproving smirk. "I'm not, and you know it. Don't try to pull any of that false shyness on me. I'm not blind. I've seen the way Mary Beth Evans and Sally Ann Crammer—to mention only a couple of your admirers—fawn all over you on Sundays—before, during and after church."

A hint of guardedness entered his voice. "Maybe I just don't like the it'll-be-a-challenge-but-*I*-can-change-him look in their eyes."

"No, I suppose you wouldn't," she conceded, her gaze traveling to the empty fireplace. He had his rough points, but she'd settle for him just as he was, if only he loved her.

"What would you change about me, if you could, Maggie?"

The question startled her. Glancing back toward him, she found him watching her, his face unreadable.

I'd want you to love me, she answered mentally. Aloud she said, "For our child's sake, I wish you were more tolerant of my grandfather." Anger flashed in his eyes. He thought she was accusing him of being the bad guy. She added quickly, "And I want him to be more tolerant of you."

His eyes again became indecipherable as his gaze narrowed on her. "And what about you, Maggie? Are you willing to be more tolerant of the Colberts?"

Her jaw tightened. "I have always tried to be fair."

The anger returned. "Did you honestly think you were being fair when you sided with your grandfather over Wild Horse Canyon?"

"My grandfather had a legitimate claim to the canyon," she said, adding tersely, "I never said I thought he was doing the right thing, but he did have a legal right to act on that claim."

"I suppose," Joe replied, returning his attention to the saddle.

Maggie stared at him in shocked silence. She'd braced herself for a rerun of the argument they'd had so many years ago—the one that had sent them on their separate ways.

Looking up at her surprised face, he said stiffly, "I'm practicing being more tolerant." Then he again returned his attention to the saddle.

Watching him, she found herself wishing his new-found tolerance would let him learn to love her. *That's one heck of a giant step,* she chided herself. She should just be grateful for the baby's sake and not expect any more. *I won't,* she promised herself.

Chapter Seven

Maggie frowned anxiously at the clock. The same day they told Frank about the expected arrival of the newest Colbert, Joe had phoned his parents to tell them the news. To Maggie's relief, they both greeted the announcement with good wishes. Of course, this did cause her to be even more embarrassed by her grandfather's attitude, especially when Joe's mother and father insisted on talking to her so they could personally tell her how pleased they were. But in spite of her embarrassment she was glad that at least one side of the family wouldn't be causing difficulties.

Now she glanced around her anxiously. That phone call to Joe's parents had been three weeks ago. They hadn't been able to get away from Houston at that time, but today they would be arriving for a week-long visit. They wanted to officially celebrate the news.

The guest room was so clean it practically sparkled and Helen had planned her menus with David and Susan Colbert's favorite foods in mind.

Because Joe's small four-seater helicopter would have been too full with the luggage and his parents, Maggie waited at the ranch while Joe flew into San Angelo and met their plane. Walking tensely into the dining room, she checked the table settings for the tenth time. They would be arriving in time for lunch and she wanted everything perfect.

Hearing the helicopter land, she went to the front porch to greet them.

"Maggie, darlin', you're looking spectacular," David Colbert said, giving her a hug.

"You are looking wonderful, dear." Susan echoed her husband's sentiments as she, too, gave Maggie a hug.

Welcoming them, Maggie realized that in the back of her mind she hadn't quite believed their enthusiastic acceptance of her pregnancy. But seeing them face-to-face, she had to admit that they did look genuinely happy.

During lunch, Susan insisted that Maggie and Joe come to Houston when it was time to buy all the necessities for the baby. "Those stores won't know what hit them by the time Maggie and I are through," she said with a laugh.

"And I think we should have a party to show off our newest daughter-in-law," David added, beaming at Maggie.

Maggie flushed with pleasure and wished her grandfather could be as accepting of Joe. It would certainly make her life a lot easier.

The next few days passed just as nicely. Joe's parents treated Maggie like a daughter and a deep anger toward her grandfather began to fester inside of her.

Before Joe's parents arrived, Maggie had asked Frank if he thought he could behave well enough to come over for dinner one evening. Frank had thought about it, then decided it would be best if she told them he was feeling a bit under the weather. "Don't think I could stand to

be in a whole room full of Colberts," he'd said.
"Besides, I remember that David real well. When
he first became a lawyer, he tried to pull some
legal shenanigans to help his dad get some of our
land on the west range." Frank had grinned
widely. "Didn't work, though."

"I wish you would put those old injuries
aside," Maggie argued. But it hadn't done any
good.

Now as she rode over to visit her grandfather,
she was furious with him. Normally she visited
him at least a couple of times a week, but she
hadn't this week. She'd been too busy with Joe's
parents. And besides, she knew she'd end up
fighting with Frank—she was so angry with him
for his inability to let bygones be bygones. But
Sarah insisted when she called this morning that
Maggie come see her grandfather.

"He's worried about you. He wants to be certain Joe's parents are treating you well," the
housekeeper had explained, then added in warning tones, "He's threatening to ride over and see
for himself if you don't come over here."

Maggie capitulated. Joe's parents were leaving tomorrow and she didn't want their visit to
end on a sour note. She told them that her

grandfather was feeling particularly badly and she thought she should go check on him.

"You go right ahead, dear," Susan had said. "We were just planning to relax and spend the day around the house anyway—maybe go for a short ride."

Reaching the Double R, Maggie took a couple of calming breaths as she dismounted at the corrals and walked toward the house.

"Well, you don't look any worse for the wear," Frank said, coming out onto the back patio to greet her.

"There hasn't been any wear," she informed him tersely. "Both David and Susan have been wonderful to me."

"Glad to hear that—if it's the truth," Frank replied.

Maggie had been walking with him into the house. Now she stopped dead in her tracks. "You are the most bullheaded man I have ever known. Everyone else is ready to call an end to this feud and you insist on refusing to a truce!"

"I'm just not as trusting as you are. David Colbert is a politician. His success depends on telling people what they want to hear and making them believe he believes it."

"That's the most cynical thing I've ever heard," Maggie said with a scowl. "And I suppose you think Susan is only playing along because it's what her husband wants."

"Could be," Frank replied. "I can understand Joe loving you enough that he's willing to overlook the fact that you're a Randolph, but I can't believe David Colbert could change his true colors this fast. I love you, gal, as much as he loves his son, and I'd do anything to make you happy. But I'm having a real hard time adjusting to you being married to a Colbert."

"That's because you're more thickheaded than other people," she snapped.

He studied her narrowly. "Truth is, I'm afraid those Colberts might sweet-talk you into turning against me. Or have they already done it?"

Maggie sighed in frustration. "No one can turn me against you—except you." Too furious to remain in his company, she said, "I'm going back home. I'll come see you again when you're ready to be more reasonable."

Maggie was still fuming when she got back to the White Stallion Ranch. Leaving her horse with one of the hands, she went into the house. She heard voices coming from the study, but because she still didn't feel she had her anger under proper control, she decided to shower and change before letting anyone know she was back. But as she started toward the stairs, she heard Joe saying firmly, "That really isn't going to be necessary."

Then came Susan's voice. "Really, Joe, I think you should listen to your father," she pleaded. "Maggie seems to be a really sweet girl but she is a Randolph, and while I've never believed in this feuding, it wouldn't do to take a chance on losing your child."

Maggie froze in her tracks.

"I'm only thinking of you, son," David Colbert was saying. "You have to think of Maggie as if she was one of your wild mustangs—she could turn on you and bolt at the drop of a hat."

"And you don't want the Randolphs having complete control over your heir," his mother said, finishing the thought.

"If Maggie really loves you, she'll be perfectly willing to sign this paper. All it does is guarantee shared custody of your child between you and Maggie, and in the event of your death, your mother and I would take over your position of responsibility."

"I will not ask Maggie to sign any such document," Joe stated flatly.

"Son, you're not thinking straight," David persisted. "What if something happens to you? Do you realize that Maggie and her grandfather would have sole control of this ranch in the name of your heir?"

Maggie didn't wait to hear any more. Leaving the house she found her horse, resaddled it and rode back to the Double R.

She found her grandfather in his study brooding. "Maggie, I'm sorry," he apologized, rising to greet her. "I am a stubborn old man."

"No." She gave him a tight hug. "You were right. It's always a good idea to be a little suspicious of a Colbert."

"What did they do to you?" he demanded, stepping back to get a good look at her. His face took on his fighting look. "Tell me what happened and I'll see it doesn't happen again."

Maggie shook her head. "I can handle it." She gave her grandfather another hug. "I just wanted to apologize to you."

"Ain't no apologies necessary," he assured her. "I'm just glad you saw the light."

"Me, too," she replied, suddenly wondering if Joe was as deceitful at heart as his parents were. She didn't want to believe it, but she had learned her lesson about being naive where Colberts were concerned.

Returning to the White Stallion, she managed to keep up a false front until midmorning the next day when Joe and his parents took off in the helicopter for San Angelo. Then changing into riding gear, she rode out to Wild Horse Canyon. Sitting on a boulder near the spring, she absently tossed small pebbles into the water and watched the ripples as they spread out over the surface. She wanted this child, but she feared for it, too. She didn't want it constantly torn between the two families. "I'll protect you with every ounce of strength I have," she promised, pressing her hand comfortingly against her abdomen. "I just hope I have enough."

Looking at the canyon surrounding her, she shivered, remembering the anger in Joe's eyes the day they fought over this bit of land—and the answering prideful anger in hers. "I hope I haven't made a selfish mistake," she said worriedly.

When she returned to the ranch, Joe came out of his study to meet her as she entered the house. "I was getting worried," he said. "You've been gone a long time."

"I had a lot of thinking to do," she answered tersely.

A guardedness came over his face. "What's wrong?"

Her chin tightened. "I had an argument with my grandfather yesterday."

Joe scowled protectively. "What about?"

A bitterness entered Maggie's voice. "He thought I was being naive when I told him how well I was getting along with your parents and how much they seemed to like me. We parted with angry words." Maggie paused, wondering what Joe would say.

"Frank loves you," he said, looking a little uneasy. "You shouldn't judge him too harshly."

Maggie drew a shaky breath. At least he wasn't totally like his parents. She had no doubt that David and Susan Colbert would have encouraged the rift between her and her grandfather. "I know," she said. "I learned it the hard way. When I came back here, I decided to take a shower and change before I joined you and your parents in the study. But as I started up the stairs, I heard your parents insisting that you get me to sign a paper ensuring that a Colbert would always legally own half our child." A challenge flickered in her eyes. "I didn't stay to listen to the outcome. I had an apology to make to my grandfather."

Joe met her challenge. "If you had stayed, you would have heard me tell my father that he'd better forget about that paper and that if he ever brought it up again, he would not be welcome in my home." He looked hard into her face. "We have our differences, Maggie, but I do trust you to always have this baby's best interests at heart."

Her chin trembled. "The problem is," she admitted, "I'm not sure if I trust you. Your parents had me completely fooled."

"I'm not like my parents. I swear to you, Maggie, I would never do anything I thought might cause you or our child to suffer."

Maggie studied his face. She was certain he was being honest with her. Still, she had been fooled by his father. Was she letting her love for Joe blind her to the truth? "I want to believe you," she said.

"You can," he assured her.

Later, lying on the bed, trying to take a nap before dinner, she admitted that she did trust Joe. He wasn't like his parents. He'd never hidden his feelings behind a mask of goodwill. She had the memories of their numerous heated exchanges as proof of that. And he'd never sugarcoated his motives. He'd married her for the canyon and he'd gone along with her having a child because he wanted an heir.

Suddenly Joe entered the room and came to stand by the bed. "I've decided you and I need a change," he announced.

She looked up at him dubiously. "A change?"

"We never went on a honeymoon because you needed to be here to watch over your grandfather. Now he's well. So I've decided it's time we went away for a while," he said authoritatively. "How does Hawaii sound to you?"

"I've heard it's nice," she answered, stunned by this unexpected attention.

"Then start packing," he ordered. "We leave tomorrow."

Sitting next to Joe in the airplane that was winging its way across the Pacific, Maggie still wasn't quite sure what was happening.

"I wish you would stop looking at me as if you're afraid I might have some evil motive," he said with a frown as she glanced at him out of the corner of her eye for the umpteenth time.

"I'm sorry," she apologized. "This was all just so sudden."

"I thought you were beginning to look strained," he confessed. "I know you're worried about the baby being caught in the middle of the feud, and I don't know how to reassure you that I'll try my hardest to make certain that never happens. So I thought maybe if we got away, had a change of scenery, you could at least relax a little."

"You really are a very nice man," she said.

"For a Colbert," he stipulated with self-directed cynicism.

"For anyone," she replied, and he rewarded her with a smile that left her with a warm glow.

Hawaii can be very dangerous, she decided a few days later. They were sitting on the beach in a secluded cove. Joe had been so attentive, she felt like a real bride, not just a partner in a business deal. He'd seen to it that she had breakfast in bed every day, and there was always a fresh flower on the tray. He took her sight-seeing whenever she wanted to go. In the evenings they went dining and dancing. But he was always careful not to let her get too tired. And then there was the emerald ring. Looking down at the large marquise-cut stone, she remembered finding the jeweler's box on her breakfast tray that morning.

When she had looked up at Joe questioningly, he'd said, "I never gave you an engagement ring. I thought it was time I corrected that situation."

Opening the box, she'd gasped as the sunlight streaming through the French doors caught the green stone.

"I hope you don't mind that it's not the traditional diamond," he'd said. "But the green matched your eyes so perfectly, I couldn't resist it."

"It's beautiful," she'd managed to say at last.

He'd smiled. Giving her a light kiss, he'd placed it on her finger. She'd held her breath, hoping he would tell her that he'd learned to care for her. But he hadn't. Instead, he'd said, "I want you to know how grateful I am for this child."

She'd forced a smile and called herself foolish for even hoping. *He married you to get a can-*

yon, she had reminded herself curtly. *He wasn't even interested in bedding you until he started missing having a warm body to hold.* He could never care for her the way she wanted him to. There was too much history of distrust and anger between the Colberts and the Randolphs standing in the way.

Still, as she sat next to him this afternoon on the sun-warmed beach, she glanced at him and again found herself thinking that if he loved her, they could overcome any obstacle. *Don't let the romantic beauty of this place cloud your mind,* her little voice warned. *He cares about you the same way he cares for one of his breeding mares.* With this less-than-flattering thought, she again turned her attention to the ocean that stretched out in front of her.

"Penny for your thoughts," he offered.

"I was wishing we—" she caught herself just before she said "could stay here forever," and finished with, "could have a few more days here. It's so peaceful."

"We can come back," he said, putting his arms around her and drawing her down with him as he lay back on the sand.

"We could?" she questioned as her desire for him ignited within her.

Holding her possessively, he kissed her shoulder. "I've been thinking. When it's just the two of us, we get along fine. Maybe we should make a pact not to let our families interfere with our lives and make this a permament arrangement?"

Stunned, Maggie stared at him. "Permanent?" she asked, finding it hard to believe she'd heard him correctly.

His expression became guarded as if he were afraid she might read more into this suggestion than he'd meant. "I was thinking it would be best for the child if both parents shared the same roof."

He was doing it for their child. Afraid he would see the disappointment in her eyes, she concentrated on the sand beyond his shoulder.

"Look, I don't want you to think I'm trying to force anything on you," he said gruffly, when she didn't answer immediately. "We can stick to our original agreement if that's what you want."

She drew a shaky breath. She knew she should tell him that she wanted to stick to their original agreement. The longer she was with him, the more she found herself hoping he would learn to love her and she knew this hope would only lead to frustration and disappointment. But it was difficult being rational about Joe, especially when he had his arms around her. "I think you're right. It would be best for our child if we stayed together," she heard herself saying.

"I know it will," he assured her, giving her a quick kiss as if to seal this new bargain.

The next day, as she sat beside him on the plane home, she couldn't stop worrying about whether she had made the right decision. A new thought entered her mind to torment her. What if Joe fell in love with another woman? Maggie knew she would have to let him go, but she also knew it would hurt much worse than she could even imagine. She would be much wiser to end this marriage as soon as possible, she told herself. Then she looked at Joe. It was a terrible weakness, but she wanted to stay by his side for as long as he was willing to have her there.

Chapter Eight

Maggie had hoped that the peace they found in Hawaii would linger when they returned to Texas and, to her surprise, it did. She didn't think about Joe's parents, and Frank behaved himself. In fact, one afternoon, when she was barely into her fourth month of the pregnancy and was resting in bed, she found herself actually feeling relaxed and truly at home in Joe's house. Her hand with the emerald ring lay on Joe's pillow and there was a soft smile on her lips. In spite of her best efforts not to, in this dreamlike state, she was fantasizing that Joe came in and told her he loved her.

Suddenly the fantasy vanished like a puff of smoke. She heard shouting coming from downstairs. The voices belonged to Joe and her grandfather.

"I knew this peace was too good to be true," she muttered as she got up. She followed the shouting to Joe's study. Entering, she saw her grandfather waving a newspaper in front of Joe's face.

"I can't believe even a Colbert would be so stupid," Frank was yelling at the top of his lungs. "Have you seen this land bill your father is trying to ramrod through the state legislature?"

"I'm sure my father wouldn't do anything to harm the ranchers," Joe replied, with controlled anger.

"He's a politician and a Colbert. There's no telling what he might do," Frank retorted.

"It wouldn't matter to you if what he wanted to do was good for every person in this state," Joe growled, his control slipping. "As long as it's a Colbert making the proposal, you're going to be against it!"

"That's because I know Colberts for what they are," Frank said seethingly. "You're all nothing but a pack of—"

"Stop it!" Maggie demanded before her grandfather could launch into a vindictive string of adjectives that would destroy any chance of he and Joe ever getting along.

Both men jerked around to look at her. "You should be resting," Joe said gruffly.

"It's a little hard to rest with the two of you shouting loud enough for the whole county to hear," she replied.

"Didn't mean to upset you," Frank apologized, "but you got to shout at a Colbert. Their heads are so thick it takes a loud noise to penetrate to their brain."

Maggie glared at her grandfather warningly. "You're talking about your grandchild."

"My grandchild ain't going to grow up hardheaded like a Colbert," he retorted. "I'll see to that."

"Well he certainly isn't going to grow up close minded and vindictive like a Randolph," Joe countered.

Maggie felt Joe's words as if they were a physical blow. Did he really—deep down in his heart—see her that way? Standing there, she saw her child caught in the middle of this endless feuding just as she had been. Her hand went protectively to her abdomen. "The two of you are impossible!" she hissed. Turning, she started to leave the room.

But in her haste to escape from the painful truth that there could never be any real peace between her and Joe, Maggie turned clumsily. Pain suddenly shot through her ankle and she felt herself falling. She grabbed wildly for something to stop her but her hands met only air and she landed hard on the floor.

Frank and Joe were at her side in an instant.

"Leave me alone," she screamed at them. Terror that she might have injured her baby mingled with her anger and frustration.

"I'm going to call the doctor," Joe said. "Don't let her get up," he ordered Frank.

"I won't," Frank barked back. "You just get hold of that doctor."

Trying not to give in to panic, Maggie sat perfectly still while Frank eased the boot off her foot and gently moved her ankle around. The sprain was mild. She barely felt any pain. But her ankle wasn't what concerned her, anyway. It could have been broken and she wouldn't have cared. Her baby was all that mattered. Maggie carefully pressed her hands against her abdomen as if she could hold it safe.

"How's her ankle?" Joe asked, returning to the doorway, carrying the phone with him.

"The ankle doesn't look bad," Frank answered while Maggie continued to sit silently, her face rigid.

"The doctor wants to know if you're feeling any abdominal pain," Joe said, watching her worriedly.

"Not at the moment," she answered stiffly, taking deep breaths to control her panic.

Joe relayed the message, then his mouth formed a hard line. "I'm going to bring her in for an exam just to be certain," he said into the phone and hung up.

"I'm coming, too," Frank said as Joe picked Maggie up and carried her toward the door.

Joe bypassed the cars and headed directly for the helicopter. Maggie saw his face as he lifted her into the seat and knew he was as scared as she was.

By the time they got to the doctor's office, she was beginning to feel calmer. There had been no pains, but the intensity on Dr. Jones's face as he examined her started her worrying again.

"Now don't get yourself all worked up," he said, as he finished his exam. "But I want you to go on to the hospital and spend the night there, just as a precaution."

"I want to know if my baby has been injured," she insisted.

"I honestly can't answer that," he replied, then gave her an encouraging smile and added, "It looks okay, but I don't want to take any chances. The next few hours will tell us for certain. You just go along to the hospital and get a good night's rest. You can go home in the morning."

But as Joe set the helicopter down on the landing pad at the hospital, Maggie suddenly felt sharp pains. A cold sweat broke out on her brow and she began to shiver, in spite of the noonday heat. Joe lifted her out of her seat, and she felt the wetness. Looking down at her pants, she saw blood beginning to soak the legs of her jeans.

"Frank, go get some help," Joe ordered and Maggie saw her grandfather take off at a fast clip for the emergency entrance.

"I never thought I'd see Gramps take an order from a Colbert," she murmured, the words coming out slurred as she fought to remain conscious. She started to shiver violently. "Joe, I'm scared," she confessed and tears began to run down her cheeks.

He held her even more tightly to him as he carried her swiftly toward the hospital. "You're going to be all right, Maggie," he said gruffly. "You have to be."

"What about our baby?" she asked shakily. He didn't answer but she saw the fear and anguish in his eyes.

White-coated men and two uniformed nurses came toward them with a gurney.

"She's going into shock," Maggie heard a nurse say as Joe laid her on the gurney. Vaguely Maggie was aware of being wheeled through the emergency entrance. Lights blurred as they raced her down a hall.

"You can't come in here," she heard someone saying, and then heard both Joe and Frank protesting.

It's probably the only time in their lives when they're ever going to want the same thing, she thought bitterly, then lost consciousness.

"You're all right, Maggie. You're in the recovery room," a female voice was saying to her over and over again, when she next became cognizant of the world. Maggie wrinkled her face in her effort to concentrate. What was she recovering from? she wondered. Then she remembered. "My baby. Is my baby all right?" she demanded.

"You're lucky to be alive," the nurse replied. "You need to rest now and let the anesthetic wear off."

Maggie knew then that she'd lost the baby. Tears blurred her vision, then the residual effect of the sedative hit her and she dozed again.

Vaguely she was aware of being moved into a private room. Joe and her grandfather were there. But the anesthetic hadn't totally worn off and again she dozed.

Several hours later, she finally awoke from the fog to a terrible sense of loss. As her gaze traveled around the hospital room, she saw Joe asleep in the lounge chair beside the bed. Even asleep, he looked tired.

As if he could feel her eyes on him, he shifted, then woke. "Maggie?" he said rising and coming to stand beside the bed. He looked like he'd been through hell. His face was drawn and lines of strain were etched deep into his features. His eyes were puffy and she wondered if he had actually been crying. "I'm so sorry."

He was blaming himself. She was hurting badly over the loss of her child, but she would not take that hurt out on Joe. He had wanted this baby as much as she had. "It wasn't your fault," she said. "It was my own clumsiness."

"No." He shook his head. "I never should have let Frank goad me into an argument. I'd promised you I wouldn't."

Maggie drew a shaky breath as she fought to hold back the threatened flood of tears. "You were only doing what comes naturally. People are right, fighting between the Randolphs and Colberts is so much a part of us that we can never change it."

"Maybe so," he conceded. "But I made you a promise. I should have been able to keep it."

She couldn't bear to see him hurting so badly. Her jaw firmed. "I don't want you blaming yourself," she said tersely.

"You almost died, too, Maggie." Gently, he combed the wayward strands of hair back from her face. Looking up into his eyes she saw a tenderness that made her chin tremble. "I couldn't have lived with myself if that had happened."

It's guilt, she told herself, before the weakness she was feeling could fool her into believing it was anything more.

"It would've been my fault if Maggie had died," Frank said entering the room and approaching the bed. "I promised you, gal, that I wouldn't go flying off the handle, and I did it, anyway."

"It was an accident," she said tiredly. Her grandfather looked as bad as Joe did. Obviously he'd spent the night at the hospital, too. Worried about his health, she said, "I'm fine now. I want you to go home and get some rest." Turning to Joe, she asked, "Will you fly him home?"

"I don't need Joe to fly me home," Frank said before Joe could respond. "I've already made arrangements to get myself back to the ranch when I'm ready to go. But I'm not ready yet. I don't need any rest. I need to be certain you're going to be okay."

"I am," she assured him. She wanted to scream at him for his continued hostility toward Joe, but she knew she'd only be wasting her breath. Instead she said, "And even if you don't need your rest, I need mine, and I won't be able to get it if I have to worry about you getting sick again." Her voice took on a strong pleading quality. "Please, for my sake, go get some sleep."

For a long moment, Frank looked indecisive, then grudgingly, he said, "All right." But before he left, he turned to Joe. "You call me if she needs me," he ordered.

Joe scowled at the threat in Frank's voice. "I will," he assured him curtly.

"You make certain you do," Frank growled.

"Gramps!" Maggie said, seething with frustration, determined to stop the confrontation before it went any further.

"Sorry, gal," he apologized. "But it ain't easy to overcome four generations of distrust in a few short months."

Or even a lifetime, she added to herself. Aloud she said, "Please, just go home and get some rest."

"You call me if you need anything," he said gruffly. Giving her a hug, he left.

"I'm sorry about how my grandfather acted just now," she said to Joe when they were alone.

"There's no reason for you to apologize," he replied stiffly. Moving away from the bed, he stood staring out the window. "I'm the one who should be apologizing to you. I should never have agreed to this pregnancy. I knew something was bound to go wrong. It always does when Colberts and Randolphs try to mix.''

His words cut like a knife. He couldn't have made it clearer that he now believed they could have no future together. "You're right," she conceded but that didn't stop her from still wanting her lost baby. She'd never felt so empty. Afraid her control might slip and he might see how much she was hurting, she said, "I really need to be alone. I think you should go home and get some rest, too."

"I'm going to stick around until the doctor comes," he said without compromise.

Hot tears burned at the back of her eyes. In a few short hours her whole world had come crashing down around her. She'd lost her baby and all her hopes for the future. She was going to cry and she didn't want him to see her. "I really want to be alone," she said with a plea.

Nodding, he walked toward the door.

She was barely able to hold back the tears until the door swung closed behind him—and then the dam burst. Burying her face in her pillow she tried to muffle the body-wrenching sobs.

She didn't know he'd come back into the room until she felt the bed shift. Looking through tear-blurred eyes, she saw him sitting beside her. "Maggie, at least let me provide a shoulder for you to cry on," he said. Gently he took her in his arms.

Her pride demanded that she reject his comforting, but she was too weak. At this moment she needed his arms around her.

Maggie cried until she was exhausted, then she slept. The next time she awoke, she again found Joe asleep in the lounge chair.

Looking at him, she tried telling herself that what had happened was for the best. Joe didn't love her and a marriage bound together only by a child would never have worked. Eventually they would have parted and then no matter how hard they tried not to let it happen, the child would have felt torn between them. But all the reasoning in the world couldn't make the loss of her child any easier.

The doctor came in a while later. Joe left while he examined her. When he was finished, the doctor invited Joe back into the room so he could assure both of them that Maggie had suffered no permanent damage. "She shouldn't get pregnant for at least six months," he cautioned. "But once her body has had time to fully heal, there's no reason she can't have a healthy child."

I can think of one very good one, Maggie thought tiredly—Joe won't volunteer to father another one. He'd made that clear this morning. Outwardly she smiled weakly and thanked the doctor.

"I'm glad you're going to recover fully," Joe said when they were alone.

Even the relief on his face didn't totally mask the guilt he was still feeling. Anger mingled with regret and frustration. "It's been a long night," she said. "And an even longer morning. I think you should go home and get some rest now."

"Yeah," he agreed. Still, he hesitated. Watching her uneasily, he said gruffly, "I'm really sorry about the way this worked out."

She wanted to scream at him that she didn't want his apology and she didn't want him to feel guilty. It wasn't his fault he didn't love her. It wasn't his fault she lost the baby. It had been an accident caused by her own clumsiness. But instead, she repeated what she had been trying to convince herself all morning, "Maybe it's for the best."

"Yeah, for the best," he said and left.

Closing her eyes, Maggie tried to shut out the world. But the world refused to be shut out. Almost the moment Joe was gone, she heard her door swing open again. This time it was Jane. Maggie moaned inwardly when she realized that Joe had hired the private-duty nurse. She was in no mood to be watched over like a baby chick.

"I am so sorry for you and Joe," Jane said with honest sympathy as she approached the bed and deftly took Maggie's blood pressure and pulse. Pulling the covers up around her patient, she smiled encouragingly as she added, "But you mustn't dwell on what can't be changed. We have to concentrate on getting you healthy again. Now you just rest. I'll be right here if you need me."

Maggie didn't want to hurt the woman's feelings, but she wanted to be alone. "I appreciate you agreeing to take this job, but I really don't need a private-duty nurse," she said firmly.

"You know that and I know that and the doctor knows that," Jane agreed with a reassuring smile. "But your husband insisted. And you have been through quite a trauma." Her voice took on an authoritative note as she added, "I do hope you aren't going to be as difficult a patient as your grandfather was.''

It was clear that arguing would be useless. ''No,'' Maggie replied and, closing her eyes, she again tried to sleep.

The next time she awoke, she found a huge bouquet of roses on the table beside the bed.

''They're from Joe,'' Jane said. ''You're so lucky to have a husband who cares so much about you.''

If he loved her, she would've felt like the luckiest woman in the world, Maggie thought bitterly. As it was, she took no pleasure in the flowers.

When Joe came back that evening, he brought her a complete dinner of her favorite foods. ''Jane told me you weren't eating,'' he said, standing beside the bed. ''You have to rebuild your strength. If you don't eat this, Helen is going to be real angry.''

Even Helen's food didn't tempt her. She was too depressed. ''I'm really not hungry.''

''If you're determined to be stubborn and not eat, then I'll have to feed you myself,'' he threatened.

She could almost hear him thinking that she was a true Randolph and stubborn as a Missouri mule. Tossing him a haughty glare, she picked up the fork and ate.

From then on, whenever she didn't eat everything on her hospital tray, he brought her a meal from the ranch and stood by the bed and watched her eat it.

He also brought her a stack of magazines to read and a fresh bouquet of flowers arrived every day. Determined to keep his attentions in the proper perspective, she constantly reminded herself that he was only doing this out of guilt.

But when she returned to the ranch a few days later, she was surprised to find the nursery still intact. She wondered if Joe regretted what he'd said right after the loss of their child and had changed his mind about their trying for another one. In spite of what she'd said and thought while lying in the hospital, she knew she would agree if he asked her.

"I thought you would have already changed this back into a guest room," she said when Joe found her in it.

"I started to, but Helen insisted on letting it stay a nursery," he replied uneasily. "She kept pointing out that the doctor said you would be able to have more children. I didn't feel I could tell her we weren't planning on any. That would've only led to questions we wouldn't want to answer."

You stupid fool, Maggie chided herself. *You'd think you would have learned by now that hoping, where Joe is concerned, is only going to cause you pain.*

Standing in that room that day, she very slowly and very carefully constructed a protective shield around herself. There would be no more hurting, she promised herself.

But it wasn't easy to block out her feelings. In the bedroom, they moved back into their neutral corners and she told herself she was happy with this arrangement. But late in the night she would wake up and ache to be in his arms. She began to sleep badly, fearing that in her sleep she would move over toward him.

She noticed Joe had circles under his eyes, too. No matter how hard he tried to hide it, it was clear that her continued presence under his roof was a strain. Maggie's old feeling of being a nuisance in his home grew stronger with each passing day.

Then one hot September day, about seven weeks after her miscarriage, she found Joe in the nursery staring down into the empty crib.

Seeing her, he straightened and turned toward her accusingly. "I wanted the child," he said tersely. "But I wanted it for all the wrong reasons. A child should be born from love and for no other reason." There was a deep brooding anger in his eyes. "You were right about one thing, Maggie. I do want a family. But I want to have it for all the right reasons, not the wrong ones." Brushing past her, he left the room.

He didn't need to spell it out for her. She understood what he was saying. He wanted a wife he loved and she was standing in his way. It was time for her to call an end to this farce of a marriage.

Packing her suitcases, she toyed with the idea of catching the first plane to anywhere, but the fear that Joe would guess how much she cared made this only a fantasy. She would play this out with dignity and coolness. He would expect her to go back to the Double R, so that was where she would go for the moment. As she snapped the suitcases shut, the green glint of the emerald on her finger caught her eyes. "Forever turned out to be much shorter than I expected," she said with a tired sigh. Slipping it off, she laid it on top of the bureau. Then she slipped off her wedding ring and laid that beside it.

That done, she picked up her suitcases, carried them out to her car and loaded them into the trunk. Then after sending one of the hands to find Joe and tell him she needed to speak to him, she went into his study and waited. It wasn't an easy wait. She always felt his presence strongly in this room. Almost as if it were yesterday, in her mind's eye, she saw him cleaning the child's saddle. With that image came the sharp memory of their encounter in the nursery only an hour earlier, and her jaw tightened. She would leave here and put him behind her for good this time.

"Jack said you wanted to see me," Joe said as he entered the room. He looked uncomfortable, and she knew their earlier confrontation was still on his mind.

"I wanted you to know that I'm leaving." She repeated by rote the lines she had been practicing for the past hour. "I've decided that we both have suffered enough. It's time to end this farce of a marriage."

"I apologize for my outburst upstairs, Maggie," he said stiffly. "We have an agreement and I plan to live up to it."

That darn canyon! She'd been so caught up in her own anguish, she'd forgotten all about it. A Randolph had never gone back on a deal before. Her ancestors were probably turning over in their graves. But staying under Joe's roof was more than she could handle. He'd made it clear he wanted to find a woman he could love, and she wouldn't stand in his way. "I can't stay here any longer and you need to get on with your life. I'll try to get my grandfather to give you Wild Horse Canyon," she said tersely. "But that's all I can promise."

The scowl on his face darkened. "I don't want the canyon, Maggie. You nearly died because of me. I figure we're even on all counts." His jaw tightened. "I just don't want you ending up in another mess because of pressure from your grandfather."

The guilt again! "I won't," she assured him. "I've learned a lot from this experience."

As if a truth had suddenly dawned on him, his gaze narrowed and a cynical smile played at the corners of his mouth. "I guess you have. And, I guess I'm not the only one you want to see getting on with their life." When she frowned at him in confusion, he added curtly, "Now that you're not afraid of men any longer, I guess you'll be looking for 'Mr. Right'?"

He made it sound as if she had purposely set out to use him. Well, their relationship had worked both ways. He'd helped her overcome her fear of men and she'd helped him learn what he wanted out of life. "Turnabout's fair play," she said evenly. "You'll be out there looking for 'Ms. Right'."

"Sure will," he confirmed, his jaw tightening with purpose. Then his manner became that of one who was seeing a nuisance finally leave his life, and he said, "You need some help with your bags?"

"No, I've already loaded what I'll need for now into my car," she answered. "If you could ask Helen to pack up the rest and send it over, I'd be grateful."

"Sure thing," he said, stepping aside so she could leave.

As she slid in behind the wheel of her car a couple of minutes later, Maggie started to shake. "Darn!" she cursed as she nearly dropped the key trying to get it into the ignition. She felt like she was sixteen all over again as the pain washed over her in waves. "You promised yourself this wasn't going to happen," she scowled at the pale image in the mirror. Then, jamming the key into the ignition, she started the engine and drove away.

Frank came out to greet her as she parked in front of the ranch house at the Double R.

"You look terrible, gal," he said watching her climb out of the car.

"Thanks, Gramps," she returned with a scowl. "Always could count on you to boost my ego."

"Now don't be smart with me," he scowled. "I'm concerned about you. You've been looking pale and worn down ever since you lost that baby."

"I've left Joe," she heard herself saying bluntly. She'd meant to ease into it but her mind wasn't working very well.

"Good for you," Frank replied, placing an arm around her shoulders. "I've been sorry ever since I let you marry that Colbert boy. It ain't natural for our two families to try to mix."

"Then why does it hurt so bad?" she asked as the tears began to stream down her cheeks.

Frank folded her into his arms. "Mistakes always hurt."

Furious with herself for crying, Maggie brushed frantically at her cheeks as she stepped away from him. "I was wondering if I could have my old room back for a few days until I can make other plans."

"This is your home, Maggie," he said. "You can stay here until your dying day."

"I just want to stay for a few days," she repeated. Fighting back a fresh flood of tears, she opened the trunk and took out her suitcases.

"We'll talk later," Frank said, taking one of the suitcases and placing an arm around her shoulders as they walked toward the house. "Right now you need to rest."

Maggie nodded. She told herself she should feel relieved. She'd done what had to be done. She'd freed Joe and now she was going to put him behind her. But she didn't feel relieved. She felt as if she was being torn apart inside. Alone in her room, she lay on the bed staring at the ceiling, fighting back the tears. It was stupid to cry over Joe. But stupid or not, the tears burned hotter and hotter. Finally giving in, she promised herself one last cry and sobbed herself to sleep.

Later, as she splashed cold water on her face to take the puffiness away from her eyes before she went down to dinner, she felt more in control. It was time to look to the future. Joe Colbert was a part of her past, and she was finished with him forever.

"Sarah's going to be right angry if you don't stop playing with that food and put some in your mouth," Frank said, frowning worriedly at Maggie's dinner plate. He'd been watching her rearrange her food for nearly an hour without even taking a bite.

Flushing, Maggie quickly took a bite and swallowed. Even Sarah's food tasted like cardboard tonight.

"You mentioned some plans you're thinking of making?" Frank said, his intonation making the statement come out like a question.

"Thought I might go to college or a vocational school and learn an occupation," she answered, her jaw set firmly. "Then go find a job in Dallas or Austin."

"You ain't no city girl." Frank shook his head to add emphasis to his words. "And you've got an occupation. You're a rancher and a darn good one. I know because I'm the one who taught you. Why, you could run this ranch singlehanded."

Her jaw tightened. She wanted distance between her and Joe. "I can't stay here."

"Sure you can, gal." Reaching over, Frank took her hand in his.

Just the possibility of seeing Joe again in the near future shook her. Her jaw tightened even more. "No, I can't."

Frank's voice took on a pleading quality. "I want you here with me, Maggie. I'm an old man. I don't want to die alone."

Maggie felt torn. She didn't want to leave her grandfather, but she couldn't lie to herself. Getting Joe out of her system wasn't going to be easy. He had a way of destroying her control and she wanted the distance between them to prevent herself from saying or doing something that might make a fool of her. "I'll come back to visit often."

"You're running away, gal." Frank scowled and shook his head again. "And running away never solved anything."

"I know," she admitted curtly. "But I need to put some distance between me and Joe for a while."

Frank's expression turned black. "I can't believe what I'm hearing—a Randolph letting a Colbert run her off her land."

"That's not the way it is," she hissed. "I'm merely broadening my horizons."

"That ain't how it's going to look to folks around here. No, ma'am." Frank shook his head again. "Everyone'll be saying you're running away 'cause Joe Colbert broke your heart."

And they'd be right, Maggie admitted to herself. But she sure didn't want the whole county saying it. She knew her grandfather was right. If she left, that's exactly what they'd say. "You win," she said tightly. "I'll stay."

Frank smiled broadly. "Good girl. You made the right decision."

Remembering how she'd gotten into this mess in the first place, Maggie added, "But I'm staying on my terms. I want your promise you won't try to force a marriage on me or manipulate me in any way."

"It's hard for an old man to change his ways." Frank frowned speculatively. "Does that mean I can't do *any* matchmaking?"

"None," she replied. "I want absolute freedom of choice in my life."

Tenderness came over his face and he gave her hand a loving squeeze. "This is your home, and I want you here with me. What you're asking ain't going to be easy for me, but I'll do my best."

And staying isn't going to be easy for me, she mused. But she knew her grandfather was right. If she left, she'd only be running away. If she was truly going to get Joe out of her system, she had to stay here and face him.

Chapter Nine

But facing Joe was easier said than done. The next day she headed for her room when she saw his truck approaching. Watching from a hidden position behind the curtains as he unloaded the rest of her belongings, she called herself a coward. But just seeing him caused a dull ache inside of her.

As he carried the last box inside, she breathed a sigh of relief. He'd be leaving now. But she didn't see him come right back outside as he'd done after all the previous loads.

She was concentrating so hard on watching for him, that a knock on her door caused her to jump.

It was Sarah. "Joe asked to speak to you," she said.

Speaking to Joe was the last thing Maggie wanted to do today. "Tell him I have a really bad headache and I'm taking a nap."

"I will not." Sarah stood her ground firmly. "He's your husband and the two of you belong together. All marriages have their rough spots. My Bill and I used to fight like cats and dogs, but we always made up." A reminiscent smile spread over Sarah's face. "One of the reasons I never married again after he left me a widow was because I could never find a man who could make up as well as Bill." Then her expression became firm. "You and Joe have to talk. You can't work things out by telepathy."

"There's nothing to work out," Maggie said stiffly. "People were right. The Colberts and the Randolphs mix like oil and water."

"That's your grandfather talking," Sarah snapped.

"That's four generations of Colberts and Randolphs talking," Maggie said, correcting her.

Sarah scowled. "Well, I don't care what you say. I've practically raised you and I know when you're miserable. I'm not telling Joe any lies. You can talk to him downstairs or I'll bring him up here."

"Downstairs," Maggie said grudgingly, giving in to the inevitable.

Joe was waiting in the entrance hall by the boxes he'd carried in. "Just wanted to be sure you got this. The bride's supposed to have it," he said, his face and voice were without expression as he extended the large envelope toward her. As she accepted it, a flicker of sarcasm appeared in his eyes. "Thought you might want to have the pleasure of burning it." Turning away abruptly, he left.

Sarah had been standing at the top of the stairs. Now she came down to stand beside Maggie and frowned at the envelope. "What's in it?"

Opening it, Maggie found her and Joe's marriage certificate. It was tied with the faded blue ribbon. Drawing a shaky breath, she could almost hear him saying, "I keep it to remind myself that the Colberts and Randolphs can never be anything at heart but enemies." Now the rib-

bon was tied around the marriage license as if to
add a final "I told you so" to their parting.

Maggie frowned at the housekeeper. "Now are
you satisifed that it's over between Joe Colbert
and me?"

"I'm satisified that the two of you are too
bullheaded to ever work out your differences,"
Sarah said grimly. With a shake of her head, she
headed toward the kitchen.

Maggie's chin trembled. *If he loved me, I'd
work anything out with him,* she thought sadly
as she looked down at the document in her hand.
But he didn't and he never would! Shoving the ifs
out of her mind, she picked up the nearest box
and carried it upstairs.

Late that same night she went down to the living room and started a small fire in the fireplace. But as she extended the marriage certificate toward the flames, and it started to catch
fire, she pulled it out and snuffed out the burning corner. Furious with herself for her weakness, she carried it back upstairs.

Over the next few days she settled back into
life at the Double R. She even managed to put
Joe out of her mind every once in a while. *And*

eventually, he'll be gone forever, she promised herself.

Then Sunday came. She considered pleading an illness and skipping church but if she did, the gossip was sure to fly. Everyone would be certain she had stayed home to avoid Joe and that would lead to speculation that she was nursing a broken heart. "Don't want that," she said firmly to the reluctant face staring back at her from the mirror.

But it was worse than she ever expected. The word of her separation from Joe had spread like wildfire. Even those people who usually only came to church on Easter and Christmas were there this Sunday. Entering the sanctuary, she prayed silently that Joe had stayed home. But her prayer wasn't answered. Surreptitiously glancing toward the pew where the Colberts always sat, she saw his broad shoulders and rugged profile. Mary Beth Evens was seated to his left. As Sarah, Maggie and Frank seated themselves on the other side of the church in the pew normally occupied by the Randolphs, Sally Ann Crammer eased herself into place on Joe's right. Maggie felt a hard knot of jealousy in the pit of her stomach and found herself wishing that Helen was a Presbyterian rather than a Methodist. At least with her seated next to Joe one of the two women would have been kept at bay. Then angry with herself for even caring who sat beside him, she ignored the trio.

A hush had begun to fall over the sanctuary when Maggie entered, and those who normally milled around outside until the last minute were suddenly hunting for a seat. No one wants to miss the fireworks if they should start, she mused acidly, as she smiled nicely at old Mrs. Petigrew and Mildred, her spinster daughter, who had occupied this same pew with Frank, Maggie and Sarah for as long as Maggie could remember.

Protectively, Sarah and Frank sat on either side of Maggie, but Mrs. Petigrew was not to be put off. Leaning around Sarah, she gave Maggie's hand a motherly pat and Maggie's heart caught in her throat. Mrs. Petigrew was practically deaf and because of that had a habit of talking loudly. She also had a habit of saying what she thought. Please, please let her show some restraint today, Maggie prayed.

Again her prayers went unanswered. "So sorry to hear about you and Joe," Mrs. Petigrew said in a harsh whisper that carried throughout the sanctuary. "But can't say I'm surprised. Nope. Told Mildred I never thought it could last. Too many generations of feuding in your blood."

"Mother, hush!" Mildred ordered, her face flaming as all eyes swung from their pew to Joe's pew and back again.

"I ain't saying anything everyone else isn't thinking," Mrs. Petigrew snapped. Giving Maggie's hand a final squeeze, she added, "I'm not one who takes divorce lightly, but in this case I'm sure it's for the best." Then settling back in her seat, she began to hunt through the hymnal for the first hymn of the service.

The worst has to be over now, Maggie thought as she sat stiffly and wished the service would begin soon so it could end and she could go home. But as the service began, she wished she'd stayed at home, in spite of the gossip it would have caused. The worst wasn't over. Mrs. Petigrew was wrong about what *everybody else* thought. *Everyone* wasn't ready to accept the breakup as inevitable. Standing in the pulpit, Reverend Smith scanned the congregation. There was dark disapproval in his eyes as they came to rest on Sally Ann and Mary Beth.

Maggie saw Mary Beth flush and move away a little from Joe, but Sally Ann remained where she was, straightened her shoulders and tilted her chin defiantly as if to say she was merely reclaiming stolen property.

Then in a voice that echoed through the sanctuary, the reverend said, "What God hath joined together, let no man put asunder!" Thus he launched into a fire-and-brimstone sermon on the sanctity of marriage.

He must be feeling really brave this morning, Maggie mused, trying not to show any reaction. Most people found it a little intimidating to challenge either the Colberts or the Randolphs. The reverend, however, was taking on both at the same time. Of course, he does believe he has God on his side, she reasoned. And the reverend was a man who never turned from a fight if his principles or religious teachings were involved. But she knew for certain that he was going to lose this time.

As he said the benediction, Maggie prepared herself for the final gauntlet. At the end of every Sunday service, Reverend Smith stood at the door of the church to extend a personal good wish to each member of his congregation. "I hope you'll take my sermon to heart," he said, addressing Maggie pointedly as she filed out of the church with Sarah and Frank.

"There are some things, Reverend, that cannot be overcome," she replied with stiff dignity and walked on before he could say more. She was in no mood to discuss her divorce with the whole congregation trying to listen.

Once they passed Reverend Smith, Maggie would have preferred to make a run for the car, but pride kept her demeanor casual and her pace calm. A couple of times, her grandfather paused to say hello to a friend, but he did seem to understand her discomfort and didn't linger too long. Even so, it felt like forever before she climbed into the car and breathed a sigh of relief that this ordeal was over. She hoped that by next Sunday, the county's curiosity would be directed at something or someone else.

But Joe will still be around, her little voice reminded her as they drove past the church and she saw him with Sally Ann and Mary Beth still close by. Her chin trembled and again she felt the hard, hot knot of jealousy.

Eating Sunday dinner, she found herself wondering if Joe had gone home for the Sunday meal with one of the two women. He's probably having dinner with one and supper with the other, just to get himself back into circulation, she mused, and the food she had been eating suddenly felt sour in her stomach.

Excusing herself from the table, she went upstairs. She had to get him out of her mind! Finding the marriage license, she ripped it into small pieces. It didn't help.

She needed to think, and the best place she knew to do that was out on the range. Changing into riding clothes, she went out to the barn and saddled her horse. A jackrabbit scampered out of her path as she rode away from the ranch, but she didn't notice.

"There has to be something I can do," she muttered, her brow wrinkled in thought, "to get this feeling of being bound to that man out of my system."

She hadn't been paying any attention to the direction she'd taken. Unexpectedly she found herself at the entrance to Wild Horse Canyon. Suddenly she felt as if a light had come on in her brain. The canyon had to be the answer! The first time she and Joe parted had been because of their families' dispute over Wild Horse Canyon. They had married because Joe still wanted it.

When she left Joe and returned to the Double R, she hadn't mentioned the canyon to her grandfather. These past few days had been trying enough without her worrying about fabricating an excuse as to why she wanted Frank to give Joe the canyon. Besides, Joe had said he considered them even. But Maggie didn't feel even. She'd promised herself that when the time came and the ranch was hers, her first act would be to deed the canyon over to Joe. Well, she wasn't going to wait. He was going to get it now. Then she could put him out of her life for good.

She rode back to the ranch at a gallop. Leaving her horse with one of the ranch hands to rub down, she went in search of her grandfather. He was in the living room, reading the Sunday paper.

"Well, it sure is good to see the color back in your cheeks," he said with a smile.

Coming to a halt in front of him, she stood with her feet slightly apart and planted firmly. "I want something from you. If you love me, you'll give it to me without asking any questions."

Frank eyed her dubiously. "What is it?"

"I want you to deed Wild Horse Canyon to me and promise me I can do anything I want with it," she stated bluntly.

Frank blinked, then looked puzzled. "This will all be yours one day. Why's it so important for you to have the canyon now?"

"I told you, no questions," she said tersely.

Frank scowled. "This has something to do with Joe Colbert, doesn't it? What's he doing? Is he trying to get the canyon as part of the divorce settlement?" Frank's eyes gleamed with anger. "Well, if that's it, he can roast in hell. He signed a prenuptial agreement. He can't get anything from you."

"He doesn't want anything," she replied tightly. "But *I* want him to have it."

"You tell me why and I'll consider it," Frank bargained.

"No." Maggie's jaw firmed. She refused to admit to anyone how much of a hold Joe had on her heart. "Either you give it to me without an explanation or I'm packing and leaving. I'll be gone by tonight and I'm not coming back." She'd never planned to make this threat. It hadn't even entered her mind until this moment. But once it was spoken she knew she meant it.

She couldn't go on like this. She had to get Joe out of her system and if she couldn't do it by giving him Wild Horse Canyon, then she'd do it by putting distance between them until he was only a faded memory.

Frank saw the decision on her face and frowned. "You mean it, don't you?"

"Yes," she replied without hesitation.

For a long moment he continued to study her. Then levering himself into a standing position, he said, "You're more important to me than any canyon. If it makes you happy, you can have it and do with it what you want. I won't say a word."

Maggie drew a shaky breath as her grandfather headed toward his study. She'd won. Soon she would be free from any ties with Joe Colbert.

"I've called my lawyer. He'll have the necessary documents drawn up and delivered here tomorrow," Frank informed her, emerging from his den a short while later.

Maggie gave him a hug. "Thanks, Gramps, this means a lot to me."

"Are you sure you don't want to tell an old man why?" he coaxed.

"Let's just say it's a way of purging Joe Colbert from my life forever," she replied.

"In that case, it's definitely worth it," he said with a bright smile.

The next day, Maggie called the lawyer twice and paced the living-room floor until she almost wore a path in the rug. Finally about midafternoon the lawyer showed up with the papers. It only took a few minutes for the legal matters to be taken care of and then, with deed in hand, Maggie rode to the White Stallion.

"You should have just come right in," Helen said, when she discovered it was Maggie knocking on the door. "This is still your home."

"It's Joe's home," Maggie corrected.

"I'm planning on the two of you getting back together," Helen replied firmly as she led Maggie into the living room. "And soon. That Sally Ann Crammer is driving me crazy. She's got that high-pitched giggle that just penetrates the brain, and she's been here twice already today looking for Joe with one stupid excuse or another."

Maggie felt her stomach start to knot, and her hand closed tighter on the envelope she was holding. "Joe and I aren't going to get back together," she said tersely. Before Helen could try to persuade her differently, she said, "But I do need to talk to him."

"He's not here. He went out to check on some of the fences," Helen replied apologetically, then added coaxingly, "Why don't you come into the kitchen and visit with me while you wait. Sometimes it helps to talk about a problem."

Maggie shook her head. She wanted to hand Joe the deed herself, but she was in no mood to put up with Helen's attempts to mend a marriage that should never have been in the first place. "I really can't stay. I'll just leave these papers with a note for Joe on his desk in the study."

"I may be in the minority, but I still think the two of you are making a big mistake." Shaking her head as if she found their hardheadedness close to intolerable, Helen went back into the kitchen.

As she went into the study, memories assailed Maggie. For a moment she found herself wanting Joe's arms around her just one last time. Furious that she should have this thought, she found a piece of paper and a pen. "*Now* we're even," she wrote, and clipping the paper to the envelope holding the deed, she left.

Frank came out to meet her as she drove up to Double R. "I don't want you to go accusing me of matchmaking, Maggie," he said. "But Stu is coming to dinner tonight. He called and said he wanted to come over to see you and I felt it was only polite to invite him to dinner."

Maggie decided it would be unfair to get angry. After all, her grandfather had given her Wild Horse Canyon. A simple dinner with Stu Gibson wouldn't do any harm. "I don't mind, as long as you don't start humming the wedding march," she replied.

Frank smiled with relief. "If I promise to refrain from doing any whistling or humming, will you wear a dress?" he bargained.

"I'll wear the dress, but I'm not marrying Stu Gibson," she said flatly.

"Never say never," Frank cautioned. "He's certainly different from either of your husbands. You might want to consider that. If you give him a chance you might find he's just the right sort of man for you."

Maggie rewarded her grandfather with a don't-press-your-luck look and went inside. But while she dressed for dinner, she did consider what he'd said. The man she loved didn't love her and never would. If she didn't want to spend the rest of her life alone, Stu might be a good choice. If the rumors about him were true, and she believed they were, he wouldn't be a demanding husband. This thought brought back a sudden rush of memories of the passionate nights she'd spent with Joe and a deep desire filled her. *Stop it!* she ordered herself and finished dressing hurriedly.

Stu arrived dressed in a suit and tie, and carrying candy and flowers for Maggie. Clearly he'd come courting.

During dinner he discussed ranching with Frank, but Maggie detected an impatience behind his polite facade. Frank apparently did, too, because almost as soon as the meal was over, he said, "I know you want to speak to Maggie. I'll leave the two of you alone."

Stu didn't contradict him. But, as always, he was courteous. "Thanks for dinner," he said with formal politeness, adding, "Tell Sarah it was delicious."

Frank nodded and strode out.

Stu looked like a man with a purpose when he turned back toward Maggie. "It's a nice night out, I thought we might step out onto the back patio."

Maggie nodded. She'd promised herself she would at least give Stu a chance.

The night smelled of horses and sagebrush and a crescent moon shone brightly in the clear sky. Leaning against one of the pillars that supported a partial roof, Maggie looked up at the stars. It was a night for lovers. *But I haven't had any luck with love,* she mused and turned her mind back to Stu.

"I'm a man who likes to take things slow, bide my time," he was saying. "But in this case I'm not going to wait. I waited too long last time and you married Joe Colbert."

"I'm not too sure you should go on," Maggie cautioned. She had expected a little sweet talk but this sounded like it was leading to a marriage proposal and she wasn't ready for that yet. "My divorce hasn't even been filed yet."

Stu stiffened. "Are you saying this separation might not be permanent?"

"Oh, it's permanent all right," she assured him.

Stu breathed a sigh of relief. "Then what I have to say is going to get said."

Why couldn't he at least wait until we've had a real date, Maggie thought tersely, bracing herself for what was to come.

"You've always seemed to have a bit of a wild streak in you, Maggie," Stu began in a patronizing tone. "This marriage to Joe Colbert proves it. The way I see it, to you he was like the apple was to Eve in the Garden of Eden. He was the forbidden temptation. You knew you should avoid him, but you couldn't resist the adventure. However, I feel you've learned a valuable lesson and I can see a maturity I've always worried was lacking in you."

"Thanks, I think," Maggie muttered.

"And I'm sure Joe didn't understand the deep feelings you hold for your first husband," Stu continued solemnly. "That's one of the things I've always admired about you. Even though Sam is gone, your love lives on just as mine does for Evelyn."

"I'm glad to hear you found something in me to admire," Maggie said cynically.

But the cynicism was lost on Stu. "I wouldn't be here if I didn't admire you," he assured her. "And it's this loyalty to a dead loved one that makes me think you and I can build a life to-

gether. I'm sure Joe was jealous of your continued love for Sam, but I assure you, I won't be.
And I know you'll understand my continued de-
votion to Evelyn.'' He drew a heavy sigh and
looked skyward. ''I will always be devoted to
her.'' Returning his attention to Maggie, his
manner became businesslike. ''But I don't like
living alone, and I want heirs. So when your divorce is final, I'd like for you to marry me,
Maggie.''

Maggie was tempted to tell him this was the
most unromantic proposal she could ever have
dreamed up, but she held her tongue. Considering the rumors she'd encouraged about her marriage to Sam, she couldn't fault Stu for what he
said. He was being open and honest with her, he
just didn't know the truth. ''While I realize my
marriage to Joe was a mistake,'' she said evenly.
''It will take me some time to get over it. It's very
nice of you to ask, but I simply cannot consider
your proposal at this time.''

''That's fair,'' he agreed. ''Since you didn't
flatly refuse me I'll believe there's hope.'' Moving toward her, he embraced her.

Maggie knew he was going to kiss her and she
didn't turn away. The truth was, she wanted him

to kiss her. She wanted to know if another man besides Joe could stir her blood. But as Stu's lips pressed against hers, she felt only indifference. *Darn!* she cursed mentally, waiting impatiently for him to stop.

"I never thought you'd be the kind of man who'd go courting another man's wife before the divorce papers are even drawn up," a familiar male voice said, suddenly shattering the stillness of the night.

Maggie's whole body stiffened.

Jerking away from her like a kid with his hand caught in the cookie jar, Stu turned to find himself facing Joe.

Chapter Ten

"What are you doing here!" Maggie demanded.

"Came by on a little business," Joe answered, continuing to regard Stu with cynical amusement.

Stu squared his shoulders like a man ready to fight for his lady's honor. "You don't have any business here. And since your presence is obviously upsetting Maggie, I suggest you leave."

"I will in a minute," Joe replied in an easy drawl. "But first, I do have some business here." Approaching Maggie he shoved an envelope into her hands. Then moving toward the door, he said dryly, "I apologize for interrupting your little romantic tryst. Hope the reverend doesn't find out. Stu could find himself the object of next Sunday's sermon. 'Thou shalt not covet thy neighbor's wife'—at least not until the divorce papers are signed."

Recovering from her initial shock, Maggie recognized the envelope in her hand. "He can't do this to me," she hissed, starting after him, but as she reached the front door, his car drove off.

"Can't do what to you?" Stu questioned, coming up behind her. Frowning in confusion, he stared at the envelope in her hand. "What's this all about?"

"It's none of your business," she snapped. Then realizing what she'd said, she turned to him apologetically. "I'm sorry, it's just that Joe can be so infuriating. I really do have a terrible headache. Please excuse me." Before Stu could say anything, she raced up the stairs.

Entering the bedroom, she slammed the door closed. Leaning against it, she opened the envelope. Inside were the torn pieces of the deed with a note that said simply "No thanks."

"Darn him!" she seethed. He had to take it. She thought of it as his property. If he didn't take it, she'd never be rid of him.

A hard knock on her door caused her to jump.

"Maggie, what's going on?" her grandfather demanded from the other side. "I heard people stomping through the house, then doors slamming, then Stu came to tell me Joe'd been here and you'd gone upstairs with a headache."

Maggie took a couple of calming breaths, then opened the door. "He brought back the deed to Wild Horse Canyon," she explained tersely.

Surprise registered on Frank's face. "He did?"

"Yes, but he's going to take it back," she replied with angry determination.

"Wonder why he'd do a thing like that?" Frank frowned in confusion. "He's been wanting that property for as long as I can remember."

"He returned it because he's bullheaded and wants the last word no matter how high the price," she seethed. "But he's not going to get it. Now, if you'll excuse me, I need to find some tape."

Still shaking his head in confusion, Frank went back to his study.

It took her over an hour to get the deed taped back together. The clock on the wall said it was eleven. But she didn't care how late it was. She was going to return this deed to Joe tonight.

Pulling up in front of his house, she almost hesitated as it occurred to her that he might not be alone. Then her chin tightened. If he wasn't, it would serve to help her get him out of her system even faster. Reaching the front door, she banged the iron knocker with all her might.

"What the devil?" Joe growled as he jerked the door open a couple of minutes later.

It was obvious he'd been asleep. His hair was mussed and he was barefoot, wearing only a pair of jeans.

Seeing the broad expanse of bare chest, Maggie suddenly ached for him again. *No!* she screamed at herself in bitter frustration. *He doesn't want you!* She filled her mind with the memory of his rejection and a coldness spread through her. "This is yours and you're going to accept it," she said harshly, shoving the envelope at him.

"I didn't complete my part of the bargain," he responded curtly. Refusing to accept the envelope, he stepped back and started to close the door.

But Maggie was determined. Before he could act, she put her hand on the door to keep it open and stepped into the entrance hall. "In my mind you did. This property is yours and you're going to take this deed and be out of my life once and for all."

The impatient anger she knew so well was in his eyes. "And what bargain did you strike with your grandfather to get your hands on that?" he demanded. "Did you promise him you'd eventually give in and marry Stu?"

Maggie scowled with indignation. "I didn't promise him anything. I asked him for it and he gave it to me."

"Just like that? You asked him for it and he gave it to you?" Joe questioned with sarcastic disbelief.

"Yes, just like that," she replied with a snap of her fingers.

"If you're telling me the truth, what was that scene I witnessed out on the patio all about?" he challenged. "I can't believe you'd seriously consider that proposal. Sounded obscene the way he painted the picture of you and him and both your ghosts sharing the same house—the same bed.''

"You eavesdropped!" she said accusingly.

"I didn't want to burst in and spoil the moment. Not every woman gets a proposal like that," he replied sarcastically.

Maggie fought down an embarrassed flush. "You're impossible!"

Cynical amusement flickered in his eyes. "I have to admit I like being referred to as the forbidden temptation you couldn't resist."

"You are truly impossible!" Wanting only to get away from him, she shoved the envelope at him again. "Take it. It's yours."

He shook his head. "I'm not going to accept it."

Her jaw tensed until it felt brittle. "Yes, you are."

"I told you when you left that I considered us square on all counts." The impatient anger returned. "I don't understand why you're so adamant about my having the canyon."

She faced him grimly. "Because it feels like a thorn in my side. In my mind it belongs to you. It's what you've always wanted and I want you to have it.'' Unable to face him any longer, she threw the envelope at him and turned to leave.

But before she could take a step, his hand closed around her arm. Turning her back toward him, he glared down into her face. ''What I have always wanted, Maggie, was you.''

She stared at him in wide-eyed disbelief. ''Me?''

''The reason I found Stu's reference to me as your forbidden temptation so amusing,'' he continued in angry, curt tones, ''was because for years you've been mine.''

''Yours?'' she choked out, desperate to believe him.

''I was too young and too full of pride when we first fought,'' he continued harshly. ''By the time I realized what a mistake I'd made by not trying to meet you halfway, you'd already run off and married Sam Hagan. Then when you came back, you were so untouchable I gave up any hope there might be a chance for us. I tried to convince myself that what I felt for you wasn't really love, it was just lust for something I knew I couldn't have. Then this marriage business came up.'' The bitterness in his voice grew stronger. ''I saw it as a way to finally get you out of my system. I was even willing to agree to a marriage in name only. I just wanted you here with me. I figured we'd fight enough, I'd see that I was right in the first place—Colberts and Randolphs shouldn't try to mix. Then you let me make love to you and I was lost. I never knew a love could burn so strong or feel so deep."

The anger in his eyes warned her that his love had turned to scorn. Tears of frustration burned at the back of her eyes. "You never gave me any clue," she said tightly.

"I have my pride, Maggie. As it was, I let you give my ego quite a beating," he growled.

"I—" she wanted to tell him that she had also hidden her true feelings because of pride, but he cut her off. There was too much anger in him to listen to anything she had to say.

Without giving her a chance to speak, he continued tersely in a voice filled with self-directed mockery, "After the first time we made love, I laid awake for a long time trying to convince myself that it was me you were responding to, not just a new experience. During the next few weeks, I almost convinced myself you felt something for me, then you came to me with the request for a child. It was as if my being the father was secondary, a mere accident of proximity." A bitter smile tilted one corner of his mouth. "And you want to hear something really funny? Even after all that, I could have killed Stu Gibson tonight when I saw him kissing you." Releasing her abruptly, he picked up the envelope and shoved it into her hands. "Now take your damn canyon and get off my ranch and out of my life." Then taking her by the arm, he guided her out the door and closed it behind her.

Standing in frozen shock on the porch, Maggie listened to him click the lock in place. Her hands balled into fists. He might be hating her now but he had loved her. If there was any chance for them, she would fight for it with her last ounce of strength. Stepping up to the door, she banged the knocker frantically.

"Maggie, go home," Joe yelled from inside. "I've told you I don't want that damn canyon."

"What's going on?" Maggie heard Helen demanding in perturbed tones. "You two are going to rouse the whole county."

"Just tell Maggie to go home," came Joe's barked order. "I'm going back to bed."

A moment later the door opened.

"I have to talk to Joe," Maggie said in a voice that held no compromise. She didn't want to argue with Helen, but she would if she had to.

Stepping aside, Helen motioned toward the stairs. "It's about time one of you talked to the other."

"Thanks," Maggie said with relief. Passing the housekeeper, she took the stairs two at a time.

Bursting into the bedroom, she found Joe getting ready to take off his jeans.

"I'm really tired, Maggie," he said with a scowl as he rezipped the zipper and resnapped the snap. Then turning to face her, his shoulders squared. "I'm not interested in hearing any apologies from you. What's done is done. I just want it finished."

"Well, I don't," she said shakily. "Eleven years ago we walked away from one another and I've carried that pain with me to this day." Her eyes met his. "Do you really think I could have let a man I didn't love touch me, much less make love to me after all I had been through with Sam?"

Joe didn't answer. He just stood looking at her as if he wasn't certain if he could believe her.

"I thought you only wanted the canyon. When I knocked over that box of photos in the attic, you acted as if it was junk you'd just forgotten to toss away." The sharp pain of that memory washed over her and her jaw tightened. "I have my pride, too."

He studied her guardedly. "When you said you wanted a child, you seemed almost indifferent as to who the father would be."

"I wasn't." She licked her dry lips. If she wanted him, she was going to have to be totally honest. "I wanted a part of you I could love openly without making a fool of myself." Her voice became defensive as she added, "You acted indifferent yourself. You told me your only interest in our having a child was so you would have an heir." Suddenly other hurtful memories assailed her. "And it was you who said our having the baby was a mistake."

"I said it was a mistake because we wanted it for all the wrong reasons," he corrected her gruffly. "The truth is my wanting an heir was not the real reason I agreed to the pregnancy. My motives were much more selfish than that. I had planned to use the baby to keep us together."

She remembered his proposal on the beach. But if he was telling her the truth, if he wanted her, not just the child, then why had he turned away from her after she lost the baby? "If that's true," she said shakily. "Why were you so distant after the miscarriage? If you loved me, like you say, why did you treat me as if you couldn't stand to have me around?"

Pain filled his eyes. "All I could think of all the time you were in that operating room was that you might die because of my selfish conniving. I hated myself for risking your life like that." He raked a hand through his hair in an agitated manner. "Afterward, I was afraid to touch you. I didn't feel I deserved to touch you."

Her chin trembled. "I thought you just wanted to get rid of me."

"Oh, Maggie. If you only knew how much I wanted to hold you."

They had been standing a room apart. Now as he moved toward her, she ran into his arms. They closed around her and she felt whole again.

"I love you so much," she said between kisses. "I know it won't be easy dealing with our families, but I'm willing to face anything if I know you're by my side."

"I'll always be by your side," he assured her. Then suddenly his expression turned grim once again and he looked hard into her face. "But there is one other question I want answered."

She saw the edge of anger in his eyes. "What?" she asked nervously, finding courage in the fact that he was still holding her as if he was never going to let her go.

The anger burned brighter. "I want to know why you let Stu kiss you."

Relief spread through her. "You really are jealous," she said in amazement.

"That's right," he admitted. "And I want an answer."

She smiled playfully. "It was an experiment. I wanted to see if I could feel anything when another man kissed me."

"And?" he demanded.

"Nothing," she replied, kissing the hollow of his neck. "I felt absolutely nothing."

"I hope that's the end of any experimenting," he growled, moving his hands possessively along the lines of her body.

"The end," she promised.

Lifting her into his arms, he carried her toward the bed.

"There is one other little thing you should know," she said hesitantly.

He came to an abrupt halt. "What."

"I ripped up our marriage license."

"I'll send for another one," he said, continuing toward the bed.

"Don't bother." She kissed his jaw. "I kept all the pieces and I'm getting pretty good at taping things back together. I just didn't want you to be surprised when you saw it." She kissed him again. "Besides, it will be a good reminder of what can happen when we let our stubborn pride get in the way."

"In that case I think I'll have it framed," he said.

"There's a burnt corner, too," she warned.

Joe laughed softly. "Sounds like a perfect license between a Colbert and a Randolph."

"Just perfect," she agreed with an answering laugh. But as he laid her down on the bed and started to join her, she suddenly moved away from him and got off the bed.

"I have to call my grandfather," she said in answer to the question in his eyes. "He knows I came over here and if he doesn't hear from me, he'll be banging down your door."

"I wouldn't want any interruptions," Joe admitted, as she picked up the receiver of the phone on the bedside table and dialed her grandfather's number.

"Been worried about you, gal," Frank said when he heard her voice. "Where are you and when will you be back?"

"I'm at Joe's." Saying a silent prayer that her grandfather would accept what she was going to tell him, her voice took on a strong, pleading edge. "I don't want you to be angry with me, but we're going to make this marriage work. I'll turn the deed to Wild Horse Canyon back over to you tomorrow."

There was a long moment of silence on the line, then Frank said, "You keep the canyon as a gift from me to you and Joe. I'm still not sure about this marriage to a Colbert, but you've been miserable since you left him. I just want you to be happy."

Tears of relief filled Maggie's eyes. "Thanks, Gramps."

"But you just keep in mind that anytime he doesn't treat you right, you've got a place in my home," he added.

"I will," she promised.

"You will what?" Joe asked as she hung up.

He had unzipped her dress while she was on the phone and now he was easing it off her shoulders and downward. "He wanted me to remember that I always have a place to go if you don't treat me right," she replied as the dress fell to the floor around her feet.

"I plan to treat you very right," Joe assured her as he helped the rest of her clothing join the dress.

"I hope that includes my having our children for all the right reasons," she said as his touch spread fire through her body.

"After a while," he assured her. "But first you have to give your body time to regain it's strength. That's the doctor's orders." As his hands moved caressingly along the curves of her body, he added huskily, "Besides, I want you to myself for a while. After all, we do have four generations of feuding to kiss and make up for."

"I like the sound of that," she said, reaching for the snap on his jeans.

*   *   *   *   *